"Ou
stri

Blythe's voice was cold as she continued. "You were waiting for my answer about the land, Mr. Daggart. Now you have it."

Coburn's cold gray eyes bore into her. "You don't feel anything else for me? Nothing at all?"

Blythe boldly countered his stare. "Nothing."

"I've half a mind to put that to the test. But I won't." His lip curled derisively. "Don't think you've seen the last of me, though. You should know now that I never give up without a struggle."

"Are you talking about me or the business?" she asked with a disdainful lift of her fine brows.

A faint smile curved the corners of his mouth. "Perhaps both, who knows?"

Margaret Mayo began writing quite by chance when the engineering company she worked for wasn't very busy and she found herself with time on her hands. Today, with more than thirty romance novels to her credit, she admits that writing governs her life to a large extent. When she and her husband holiday—Cornwall is their favorite spot—Margaret always has a notebook and camera on hand and is constantly looking for fresh ideas. She lives in the countryside near Stafford, England.

Books by Margaret Mayo

Conflict

Margaret Mayo

Harlequin Books

TORONTO • NEW YORK • LONDON
AMSTERDAM • PARIS • SYDNEY • HAMBURG
STOCKHOLM • ATHENS • TOKYO • MILAN

Original hardcover edition published in 1989
by Mills & Boon Limited

ISBN 0-373-03029-0

Harlequin Romance first edition January 1990

CHAPTER ONE

THE sound of screeching tyres and crunching metal still rang in the air. Blythe had seen no more than a blur of red before her car was slammed against the old stone gatepost. She wasn't hurt, just shaken up and furiously angry.

Who the hell was it turning into her drive at such a maniacal speed? She didn't stop to think that she had been guilty of the same reckless driving. But she was late—and she had never had visitors at this time in the morning, and never visitors in expensive sports cars!

She watched the man unfold himself from the low-slung vehicle, catching a brief glimpse of untidy blond hair and an angular face before he straightened. All she could see now was a hard, flat stomach and long, muscular legs encased in a pair of black designer cords.

The legs came nearer and she leaned across and released the lock on the passenger door. She ought to get out instead of sitting watching him, except that she felt too stunned to move.

He wrenched the door open and narrowed, assessing, blue-grey eyes met hers. *Familiar eyes.* Eyes that had once looked tenderly into her own. The shock was even greater than the impact of the collision.

'Are you hurt?' The clipped tones held no compassion. He sounded as though it wouldn't have mattered to him if she were, and he certainly wasn't surprised to see her.

Blythe shook her head. Coburn Daggart, of all people. The man she had hoped to avoid at all costs.

5

'Do you always drive like that?'

It was an accusation, not a question. Blythe stared at him hostilely. 'Do you? Didn't it occur to you that someone could be coming out?'

'Not at such a suicidal speed.'

Her blue eyes widened incredulously. 'This is a private lane, as you well know.'

'That's no excuse for careless driving.'

'I like that!' she flared at once. 'Careless driving? Me? If you hadn't been speeding, this would never have happened.'

His thin lips compressed until they were almost invisible. Blythe noticed a muscle contracting in his jaw. He was clean-shaven and smelled of expensive after-shave. In fact, everything about him screamed money. His soft black leather jacket must have cost more than her whole wardrobe put together.

He had changed in eleven years. He had lost weight and his face had thinned until it was all angles and lines. Gone was the boastful young man. He had used words to impress her then; now his image did it for him. He was every inch the successful businessman.

'You'd better get out, Blythe,' he said sharply. 'I'll see what damage has been done.'

She eyed him with aggression, but obediently slid across the two seats, ignoring his outstretched hand, instead tugging down the skirt of her grey suit. To her dismay her legs felt like jelly and she leaned against the car for support, tossing her long brown hair off her shoulders. He frowned. 'You sure you're all right?'

Blythe nodded, ignoring the niggling pain in her head. She had banged it against the window when her side of the car rammed the gatepost. It would pass.

He walked around the car, his straight brows drawn together. Blythe watched him and could not deny that he still had a certain charisma. He wasn't particularly handsome, he never had been, but there was something about him that made him attractive to women. And she had forgotten quite how tall he was.

At five feet six she was by no means short herself, yet she had always felt dwarfed by him. Not that she was interested now. He had done the dirty on her once, and that was enough. She wondered whether he was married yet. No one had mentioned him since she came back. And she had certainly given him no more than a fleeting thought.

His voice suddenly broke into her meditation. 'I think you're lucky. It doesn't look too bad.'

She was *lucky*? What was lucky about being shoved off the road? Blythe looked at his car. A Ferrari, no less. It spoke for itself. He probably hurtled around the countryside all the time. And the only damage was a dented bumper! She felt like taking a sledge-hammer to it.

'It will be a bit tricky moving your car without scratching it further.'

'What's a few more dents?' she asked scathingly. 'You'd better get in and do it. I'm in a hurry.'

An eyebrow lifted. 'The truth at last. You were speeding. I knew it wasn't my fault.'

As he climbed across the seats Blythe glimpsed a pair of black, tooled leather boots. He had certainly achieved his ambition. He had always said he was going to be rich.

Yet it didn't look as though it had come easy. His boyish good looks had disappeared and there were lines gouged from nose to mouth that hadn't been there before. The set of his jaw suggested grim determination. It had probably been a long, hard haul, and if the way

he had treated her was anything to go by he hadn't cared
who he trod on in the process.

She winced as her car scraped against the gatepost,
and when Coburn Daggart got out the other side she
tried not to look at the gleaming bare metal staring out
from the blue paintwork, or the obscene dents in the
door and wing. 'Thank you,' she said. 'My insurers will
be in touch.'

His mouth twisted wryly. 'I'm sure we can settle this
thing far more amicably.'

'What's wrong?' flashed Blythe. 'Afraid of losing your
no-claims bonus?'

'It would be a pity,' he admitted nonchalantly, 'but
that's not my main concern. Could you afford to lose
yours?'

'I'm the innocent party,' she snapped.

'That's debatable.'

She glared at him impotently. 'You're wasting my time.
I have to go.'

'In which case I'll call round again. Aren't you curious as to why I was coming to see you?'

In truth, Blythe had completely forgotten that he had
been turning into her driveway. 'I expect you're going
to tell me.' And she hoped it wasn't to renew old ac-
quaintances. She had thrust Coburn Daggart firmly from
her mind, and that was where he was going to stay.

'Not now,' he answered with a faint smile. 'I'll see
you this evening. Maybe you would allow me to take
you to dinner?'

'No, thanks,' said Blythe tonelessly. 'You can come
at six and I'll spare you a quarter of an hour. I'm a very
busy person these days, in case you didn't know.'

'Oh, I know,' he said, his smile widening. 'Very well,
Blythe. Tonight at six.' He stood back for her to get into

her car, closing the door and then watching as she drove away.

Her mind was a frenzy of memories, suddenly and violently resurrected. She had met Coburn when she was Wassail Queen and he was the new owner of Druid's, a neighbouring cidermakers, full of self-importance because he had his own business at the age of twenty-three. He had appeared at the wassailing and all the girls had flocked around him, but it was on Blythe his eyes remained longest.

The pagan custom of wassailing was held every year in the cidermaking industry in order to ensure a heavy yield of apples. As Wassail Queen, Blythe had poured mulled cider around the roots of the trees to encourage growth, placed toast soaked in cider in their branches for the good spirits, and then stood back and watched as shots were fired into the trees to frighten away the evil spirits.

It was a time of much revelry and fun, and Blythe had been flattered when Coburn Daggart had paid her so much attention. Only sixteen at the time, she had added a couple of years to her age because she did not want him to think her immature.

She had ignored the fact that he was big-headed and boastful and enjoyed the feeling of superiority his attention had given her. All the other girls were wild with envy.

Her father had disapproved of their relationship, but she did not care. She'd fallen in love with Coburn for a few ecstatic weeks, and it was the end of her world when for no reason that she could think of he stopped asking her out.

After a few miserable days her self-pity changed to anger and then hatred. Pride forbade her to get in touch with him. She had been blind not to see what he was like. A permanent relationship had never entered his head. When she had shown signs of becoming too serious he had quickly and determinedly put a stop to it. He had made a fool of her and she hated him.

She was glad when her father suggested she go away to art college in London. The more miles she put between herself and Coburn Daggart, the better. She had no idea what he wanted to see her about now, and she felt like screaming because he had come back into her life.

He turned up at one minute to six. He had changed into soft suede coffee-coloured trousers with a matching jacket, worn with an ivory silk shirt and a pair of brown leather boots. His hair, as usual, looked as though it had been tossed by the wind. That was one thing about him that had not changed.

In contrast, Blythe had paid no attention to her appearance. She had taken off her jacket but still wore the same skirt and blue blouse. She had brushed her hair, which she kept straight and long because it was easy to manage, and dabbed her nose with powder, but that was all.

She had come back from her accountant full of despair, and spent the rest of the day worrying. Living away from home, returning only for Christmas and holidays, Blythe had not known anything was wrong. Her father had never said.

And now he was dead, and she had to decide whether to sell the cider business or whether to try and run it herself. It was possible to carry on, Roger had told her. Her father had lost interest when Kate died, but it could be built up again if she took the time and trouble to do so. But did she want to? Cidermaking had never really interested her.

She stood framed in the doorway, a slender girl, not beautiful, but attractive in her own way. Her mouth was too wide, she thought, her nose too long. Her huge blue eyes were her best feature. She looked at her visitor expressionlessly.

'I didn't expect you.'

His lips quirked. 'I'm a man of my word. You should know that.'

He was also a man who had no compunction about ending a relationship without a word. She compressed her lips and said nothing.

'I hope you've not been worrying unnecessarily about your car?' His blond brows rose slightly. 'I'll pay for the damage, it's——'

'And keep yourself in the clear?' she cut in icily, wishing him a thousand miles away. She had more important things to do than talk to him.

He shook his head, as if unable to understand her attitude. 'Does it really matter, so long as the car's put right?'

'I suppose not.' She shrugged. 'You'd better come in. I believe you have something else you wish to discuss?'

He nodded and followed her into the house, a rambling country property that was much too big for her. Blythe led him through to her father's study. Peter Berensen had run his business from here, and she could sit and talk to Coburn Daggart with the comparative safety of the desk between them.

She sat down and he took the chair she had placed ready for him, stretching out his legs, hooking his thumbs into his pockets. Blythe could have screamed at his nonchalance.

'We could discuss this better over dinner,' he suggested, his eyes widening hopefully.

Blythe made a pretence of shuffling papers on her desk. 'No, thank you. I have a lot of work to do.'

'Surely you can leave it until tomorrow? No self-respecting person works after five.'

'Maybe you don't, but I most certainly do. Will you please get to the point?' She sat back and looked at him directly. He exuded a sensuality which was difficult to ignore, and which was certainly far more potent than it had ever been in the past.

He smiled, and tiny lines fanned out from the corners of his eyes, and the crease from his nose deepened. 'Very well, Blythe. I want to buy you out.'

Blythe's mouth fell open. This was too much of a coincidence. Unless it was common knowledge that the business was ailing? Perhaps she was the only person who had been in ignorance.

'A surprise, eh?'

'You could say that.'

'Obviously you'll need time to think about my offer. I'm prepared to pay the full market value for the property and land. Your machinery—well, I'm not really interested in that. You could try to sell it separately, though it's probably worthless.'

Blythe frowned. He sounded as though he had gone into it all very thoroughly. 'Druid's Cider is doing well, I take it?'

He inclined his head. 'Exceptionally so, and I want to expand. You will give my offer serious thought?'

'Yes. Yes, I will. Actually——' On the verge of telling him what her accountant had said, Blythe decided against it. He might not know. It might be coincidence, after all. And her problems were private.

'Actually what?' he prompted with a faint frown.

'Nothing. But yes, I'll think about it.' She stood up and held out her hand. 'Goodbye, Coburn. I'll be in touch.'

He made no attempt to get up. 'You're dismissing me so soon?'

'I've already told you, I'm busy.'

'Doing what? Nothing that can't wait until morning.'

Blythe sighed. 'I really do not wish to prolong this conversation. Will you please go?'

He shrugged and lazily hauled himself to his feet. 'A pity. I thought I might have persuaded you to eat with me, after all.'

'No, thanks.'

'Very well,' he said resignedly. 'When can I expect to hear from you?'

'In a few days.'

He followed her to the front door. 'I'm sorry about your father, Blythe. He was a fine man.'

She nodded. 'One of the best.'

'You must be very lonely. I don't believe you've been back long? Where is it you've been living—London?'

'That's right.' Did he know everything about her? The thought galled. She yanked open the door. 'Goodbye.'

He smiled, as though enjoying a secret thought, and without warning kissed her full on the lips. Blythe was so shocked that she did nothing to stop him, and, although it lasted no longer than a couple of seconds, memories of other kisses eleven years ago came tumbling back.

'Goodbye, Blythe,' he said with a grin. 'I look forward to hearing from you.'

Blythe closed the door and leaned back against it. The Ferrari roared into life. The ache in her head increased.

He was so sure of himself, it was unbelievable. She ought to have slapped his face instead of standing there like a mindless idiot. And the fact that his kiss recreated sensations she would far rather leave buried made her all the more angry with herself.

It was a long time before she cooled down, and when later that evening Ben Rees came to see her she welcomed him warmly. He was a big, bluff man who had worked for her father for many years, and she needed someone to talk to, someone to take her mind off Coburn Daggart.

He frowned as he stepped inside. 'Blythe, what have you done to your face?'

Blythe gingerly touched the bruise on her temple. 'I had a slight accident.'

'It looks more than slight to me.'

She shrugged. 'My car tangled with Coburn Daggart's.'

'That maniac!'

'Precisely.'

'Was much damage done?'

She shrugged. 'A few scratches and a couple of dents. I'll take it in and get it fixed. Mr Daggart's paying.'

Ben looked surprised. 'So long as he does cough up.'

'I think he will. Would you like a cup of tea?'

'If you're having one.' He followed her through to the kitchen. 'How did you get on this morning?'

Ben had been with the firm all his life, and Blythe realised now that he must be worried about his job. He was almost seventy, yet very active and nowhere near ready to retire.

'It's not good news, I'm afraid.'

He grimaced. 'I guessed as much. How bad is it?'

She filled the kettle before leaning back against the cupboards to face him. 'Roger says it's still possible to put the firm back on its feet. But it will mean a lot of hard work. We've lost a lot of sales.'

'To Daggart,' he said grimly.

'I suppose so.' She hadn't given that much thought. 'On the other hand, I have the opportunity to sell. I'm going to have a word with Roger about it in the morning. I'm going to see Alan as well. It might be for the best.'

'It's up to you, Blythe. But I know what your father would have wanted.'

She swallowed hard and nodded. 'If only I'd known how bad things were. Why didn't he send for me? I thought that after Kate died he'd thrown himself into his work.'

Ben lifted his broad shoulders. 'You'd got your own life to lead. You were doing so well. He was real proud of you.'

'Too proud to ask for help?'

'It wasn't help he wanted, Blythe. He'd lost all interest. He just sat back and let things drift. I tried to tell him, but he wouldn't listen.'

Blythe made the tea and they sat down at the table. 'There's some chicken pie left, if you'd like some, Ben.'

He shook his head. 'I've already eaten. I hope you don't sell, Blythe. I don't feel like uprooting myself at my time of life.'

It occurred to her that, if she sold, Ben would be out of a home too. His cottage went with the job. She had forgotten that. 'Maybe it won't come to it,' she smiled.

When Blythe went to see Roger the next morning, he said that selling out to Coburn Daggart was the best thing she could do. 'If you were experienced in running the company, it would be different,' he told her. 'But you know nothing about it. It would be like jumping in at the deep end. I'm not saying you couldn't do it, but marketing's not cheap. It will cost money which you haven't got. And going deeper into debt is no answer.

If you take my advice, Blythe, you'll sell. Get out while you can still put a bit of money in your pocket.'

'I suppose you're right,' she said unhappily. 'I'll get a valuation done straight away.'

'I already have,' he said gently, pushing a piece of paper across the desk towards her.

Blythe tucked it into her handbag. 'I'm seeing Alan Ridsdale at eleven. I'll tell him to start drawing up a contract.'

Her father's solicitor was old, bald and benevolent. He smiled warmly at Blythe and shook her hand. They talked generally for the first few minutes. Alan Ridsdale had known Blythe all her life, and was genuinely interested in all that had happened to her since she left home.

'I suppose you know,' she said eventually, 'that Berry's Cider is in financial difficulties?'

He nodded.

'I've decided to sell.'

The old man grimaced. 'I'm sorry about that, Blythe. Your father would be, too.'

'I know,' she admitted sadly. 'But I don't think I'm capable of pulling it back together. I have no business experience and I can't afford to bring anyone else in. Will you handle the sale for me?'

'You'll need to advertise, of course.'

'I already have a buyer,' she said at once.

His brows lifted.

'Coburn Daggart. He came to see me last night.'

'Ah!'

Blythe frowned. 'Is something wrong?'

'Daggart's what's wrong. He's been after your father's land for years.'

'He has?'

'He most certainly has. And what a time he's chosen to put in his latest bid.'

'You think I shouldn't sell to him?'

He shrugged. 'It's up to you, of course, but your father was always most adamant about it, paranoid in fact. Daggart made some ridiculously high offers, but still your father wouldn't sell.'

'Not even after Kate died?' asked Blythe. 'According to Ben Rees, that's when he started to lose interest.'

'Not even then,' admitted Alan. 'It's my belief that it goes much deeper than anyone knows. Reading between the lines, I have a feeling that something happened a long time ago that made your father distrust Daggart.'

'I see.' Blythe sat in thoughtful silence for a few seconds. 'Maybe I ought to see what I can find out before I do anything.'

'I think that might be a good idea,' he said.

'Except that I don't know where to begin.'

'Maybe your father has some old papers that you haven't yet gone through? I don't know. It's only a feeling on my part. I wish I could be of more help.'

'You did the right thing in telling me,' she said quietly. 'I'm glad you did. What puzzles me is why Coburn's interested when our properties are so far apart.'

'Not any longer,' informed the solicitor. 'You really are out of touch, aren't you? He's been steadily buying up land over the years until now he owns everything around you. You're actually sitting in the middle of his estate.'

Blythe's eyes widened. 'No wonder he wants to buy me out. I didn't realise that. I saw the orchards, but somehow it never clicked. There's so much fruit grown around here that I didn't really take much notice.'

'Well, now you know. I wish you luck in your search, Blythe. And don't let him harass you. I'm always here if you need help.'

'Thanks, Alan,' said Blythe, getting up and taking his outstretched hand. 'I can't believe he only offered me the market value when you say he offered my father more.' A tiny frown creased her brow. 'He must think I'm a pushover.'

'He probably does,' agreed the solicitor. 'I'm glad I was able to advise you, even though I can't tell you the whole story. I shall be interested to hear what, if anything, you find out.'

The first thing Blythe did when she got home was seat herself at her father's bureau in his bedroom. It was no good looking through the papers in his office, because they were purely to do with the business. These were personal papers which she had not yet had the courage to sort out. It was like prying into his private life.

Tears came to her eyes when she read the love-letters her mother had sent Peter before they were married. She had not realised he was so sentimental as to keep them. Tied up in pink ribbon as well.

Blythe could not remember her natural mother. Pamela had died when Blythe herself was only three. Peter had remarried a couple of years later and Blythe had grown to love Kate as if she were her real mother. Now here were the letters from Pamela, beautiful, touching letters, penned carefully in fine black handwriting. This was a real love story. Her father must have been devastated when she died.

Carefully Blythe put them away, then went downstairs to make lunch. Not that she was hungry, but she couldn't bring herself to touch any more of the papers yet. She was choked with emotion and felt that she ought not to be doing this.

The phone rang as she was nibbling a cheese sandwich.

'Hello, Blythe,' said a deep male voice.

She frowned. 'Coburn?'

'Right in one. I wondered whether you'd come to a decision yet?'

Her tone was distinctly icy. 'I told you a few days.'

'Does it really take that long to make up your mind?'

'It's not the sort of decision one makes lightly.'

'Nor is it one to make alone. How about if I pick you up tonight and we'll talk about it over dinner?'

Blythe pulled a face. 'You're very persistent.'

'You'd noticed?' He sounded as though he was grinning.

'But the answer's still no. And by the way, I got an estimate for my car today. It's going to cost you a lot of money. New wing panels and a new door just for starters.'

'Simply send me the bill,' he said airily. 'Better still, I'll come round and give you a cheque personally. What are you doing for transport meanwhile? I could lend you a car.'

'No, thanks,' she returned coolly. 'The garage is lending me one. Goodbye, Coburn.' And she put down the phone.

It rang again immediately and she snatched it up. 'I said goodbye. What the hell do you want now?'

'Blythe?'

Her eyes widened. This wasn't Coburn Daggart's voice. 'I'm sorry, yes, who is this?'

'Who do you think it is? It's Bruce. Have you forgotten me already?'

'Oh, Bruce, I'm sorry. I'm just a bit flustered at the moment.'

'Not used to the world of business, eh?'

'You could say that. How are you, Bruce? How are things in London?'

'Dull now my best girlfriend's left.'

'Oh, yes?' she mocked. 'How about Megan and Patty?'

'They're no substitute for you.'

'But they are looking after you?'

The four of them had shared a house which actually belonged to Megan. Sometimes it had been hilarious. Bruce came in for a certain amount of leg-pulling living with three girls, but on the whole things had worked out very well. The girls had a resident handyman to do their repairs and decorating, an escort if their date stood them up, and security against unwanted callers. Bruce in his turn got his meals cooked for him, his laundry done, and a sympathetic ear if he was having girl trouble. He favoured Blythe if any of them, but she always insisted on keeping their relationship strictly platonic.

'They're feeding and watering me, if that's what you mean,' he said. 'But I'm missing you, Blythe. When are you coming back?'

Last night she might have said soon. Today she was not so sure. 'I have a business to run, Bruce.'

'You're serious about it, then? I thought you might change your mind.'

'Somehow I don't think so,' she said.

'Can I come and see you? I have some holiday due and I've never been to Somerset.'

'Of course you can, Bruce,' she said at once. 'Just let me know when.'

Blythe finished her sandwiches and drank her coffee, then went out for a walk. She needed some fresh air. Her head had begun to ache again after speaking to Daggart. It was probably psychosomatic but, whatever, she wasn't feeling too good.

Beyond the boundaries of her own property, Blythe surveyed the endless acres of apple orchards. Why hadn't she noticed them before? Why hadn't she realised that all of this had not been here when she went away? Some of it had been open fields, farms, grazing land. Now Daggart had bought it all up—as he wanted to buy her land! Her mouth set. She was surrounded by him—as far as the eye could see in all directions. It was too much to take in.

She heard the car before she saw it. She recognised the distinctive roar of the engine. Coburn Daggart braked when he spotted her. His face was wreathed in smiles as he climbed out. 'What an unexpected pleasure.'

There was no answering smile on Blythe's lips. She noticed bitterly that his front bumper had already been replaced. 'I trust you weren't about to pay me another visit?'

'Unfortunately not. Though if you'd care for a lift I'd be more than willing.'

'No, thanks,' she said tightly.

A sudden gust of wind lifted her hair, revealing the bruise she had taken great pains to hide. He frowned. 'That looks nasty.' He held back her hair with surprisingly gentle fingers, inspecting the swelling more closely.

'It's all right,' she snapped, snatching away. But the sudden movement sent a searing pain through her head and she winced.

Coburn Daggart's eyes narrowed angrily. 'You should see a doctor. Come, I'll take you.'

'It's just a bruise,' she demurred. 'Stop fussing.'

'Then at least you should rest instead of wandering around like a lost soul. Jump in. I'll take you home.'

He gripped her arm and Blythe was given no choice. She had never been in a Ferrari before. She felt very low on the ground with her legs stretched out in front of her, and she could smell the leather upholstery and the luxury—and Coburn's exclusive aftershave!

She put her head back and closed her eyes, even letting him fasten the belt around her, holding her breath while he did so because his nearness resurrected feelings she had thought dead and gone for ever. It was madness under the circumstances. It was insanity feeling total awareness of a man whose only interest lay in her estate. He had made it clear a long, long time ago that he wasn't interested in her.

CHAPTER TWO

BLYTHE lay on her bed with an ice pack on her head. Coburn had wanted to send for the doctor, but she would not let him; she did not even allow him into the house. It annoyed her that she should fall prey once again to his sex appeal. What on earth was wrong with her? Hadn't she learned her lesson?

She had lived with Bruce for five years and never felt a thing. So what had this hateful man got that Bruce hadn't? Bruce was charming, pleasant, kind, helpful, with none of Coburn's abrasive qualities. He was by far the better man.

Angrily she pushed both men out of her mind, thinking instead about the letters Pamela had sent to her father. They were tender and evocative, and her mother must have loved him very much. Would she ever love a man in that way? Pamela's heart and soul had been in those letters. It was no wonder her father had kept them.

Blythe's head was still aching over an hour later when the doorbell rang. She went wearily downstairs and her eyes widened in disbelief when she recognised her caller. A small dapper man with thinning grey hair and gold-rimmed spectacles. 'Dr Fullerton!'

'Blythe,' he acknowledged with a sympathetic smile. 'I hear you've had a nasty knock on the head. May I come in?'

'Damn Coburn Daggart!' she grated. 'I told him it was nothing, that I didn't need you. I'm sorry he's fetched you out on a wild-goose chase.'

'Let me be the judge of that,' he said mildly. And after he had examined her he announced that it was as well he had been called. 'Slight concussion, nothing serious, but you need rest. You're here alone, aren't you?'

Blythe nodded, then wished she hadn't when the pain became more intense.

'Is there someone who can look after you?'

'I'm sure that's not necessary,' she demurred.

'You can't run a business in your condition.'

'I'm not doing very much at the moment,' she told him. 'Just sorting things out.'

'Which probably means poring over papers for hours on end. It's not on, Blythe. I don't want you to do anything for the next three days at least, not a thing. Promise me?'

Blythe heaved a sigh. 'I suppose so.'

'Ben Rees's wife—will she come in and cook your meals?'

'You have it all worked out, don't you?' she asked with a rueful smile.

'Peter would want me to take every care of you.'

'I miss him,' she said sadly. 'I've never been in this house when he wasn't here.'

'We all miss him,' admitted the doctor. 'He was well-liked.' He wrote out a prescription and handed it to her. 'I expect Ben will get this made up for you. Take the tablets three times a day before meals. I'll let myself out. Goodbye, Blythe.'

Blythe sat for a few moments after Dr Fullerton had gone. This was all Coburn's fault. If he hadn't been driving so fast, it would never have happened. But she couldn't rely on Ben and his wife. It wouldn't be fair. She wasn't that ill.

A few minutes later, though, her back door was pushed open and Ben came ambling in, a worried frown drawing his grizzled brows together. 'I've just seen the doc. I'm glad you sent for him. I knew that bruise looked nasty. Where's the prescription? I'll go and get it made up.'

'You're very kind,' smiled Blythe. 'I hate putting you to this trouble. I'm sure it's not necessary.'

'If Joe Fullerton says it is, then it is,' he admonished firmly. 'Betty's got a beef casserole in the oven, she'll bring you some up for your tea. Don't you do a thing. Betty will do your cleaning and washing. And when I come back from the chemist you can tell me how you got on yesterday with Roger Coghlan.'

He was not away long, and he made Blythe a cup of tea and they sat on the lawn at the back of the house, the warm June sunshine toasting their faces.

'Are you still going to sell?' he asked, after a few minutes of sitting in silent contemplation.

Blythe had been watching a kestrel hovering far above them, its keen eyes searching out its prey. Now she turned to look at Ben. He looked suddenly tired and old, and she smiled comfortingly.

'Roger told me to sell, but Alan—you know Alan Ridsdale?' Ben nodded. 'He said to give the matter some thought. Did you know Coburn Daggart had tried to buy my father out?'

Ben's lips thinned. It was obvious he didn't think very much of this younger man. 'I heard a rumour.'

'He made several offers, in fact. And always my father refused.'

'Rightly so,' he growled. 'That damn Daggart's nothing but bad news.'

Ben looked like a ferocious grizzly bear, and Blythe could not help smiling. 'He's certainly made an impact on this area. I never realised he'd expanded so much. He's bought an awful lot of land.'

'Some people were glad to make a bit of money,' snorted Ben. 'But not your father. He thought more of his cider farm.'

'Alan seems to think there was some other reason he wouldn't sell. Do you know anything about it?'

'Can't say I do,' he replied, pursing his lips thoughtfully. 'Nothing I've heard of. But I'll tell you this, Blythe—if it was my land, I wouldn't sell to Daggart either. I remember when he first came here. Cheeky young upstart, that's what he was. You went out with him a few times, didn't you? Your father didn't like it, not one little bit. Is it him who's made you the offer?'

'Yes,' admitted Blythe, surprised to hear that her father had confided in Ben. He must have felt more strongly about her seeing Coburn than she had realised.

'You just mind what you're doing, then,' said Ben, his pale eyes worried. They were silent for a moment, each deep in their own thoughts, then he pushed himself to his feet. 'I guess I must be off, but don't forget, Betty will be round with your tea. You just stay right where you are.'

Blythe closed her eyes after Ben had gone, dozing on and off, feeling a fraud, even though she had only herself to answer to—and what did it matter if she sat and did nothing? It was a slack time of year for them, when the apples were growing on the trees and there was nothing very much to do until they were ready to be picked. If the business had been run as it should, there would be orders to execute, but their books were practically empty.

Betty brought the beef casserole, which was delicious. She washed up and bustled around the house, plumping a cushion here, straightening a curtain there. She was very much like her husband, tall and big-boned with greying hair and a comfortable smile.

'There you are, my dear,' she said. 'You've nothing to do now. I'll come and see to your breakfast in the morning just as soon as I've fed Ben. Now don't you get up till I come. I've got a key. Your father always insisted we keep a spare.'

'You're very kind,' smiled Blythe.

'Nonsense,' said the woman briskly. 'I nursed your father, I can easily nurse you. I'll be going now. Oh—it looks as though you have a visitor.'

Blythe glanced through the window and mentally groaned. A long, low red car had just pulled up outside. 'It's Coburn Daggart,' she said grimly. 'Tell him I don't want to see him, will you, please?'

'Of course,' agreed Betty at once.

But whatever the woman said, it made no difference. He strode determinedly into the house, Betty hovering helplessly behind him.

'I'm sorry, Blythe,' she said, a worried expression on her lined face, 'but he was most insistent.'

'Never mind,' Blythe smiled reassuringly. 'I doubt he'll stay long.'

'Remember the doctor said you've got to rest.'

'I will,' said Blythe. 'Thank you, Betty. I'll see you in the morning.'

The moment Betty had gone, and before Coburn had time to speak, Blythe rounded on him angrily. 'You had no right sending for the doctor. I told you it wasn't necessary.'

'And from what Betty just said, it appears it was,' he barked tersely. 'What did he say?'

Blythe lifted her shoulders. 'A bit of concussion,' she admitted reluctantly.

'As I thought. Who's looking after you, that woman?'

'Betty's calling in each day, yes.'

'But otherwise you're on you're own?'

'So?' she enquired caustically. 'I'm not an invalid. All I have is a teeny bump on my head.'

'Which needs careful monitoring. I think you'd better move into Druid's Cottage. My housekeeper will——'

'Move in with you?' cut in Blythe angrily. 'You must be joking. What's wrong, is your conscience bothering you? You've decided it's your fault after all, and you see this as some way of making up?'

His eyes narrowed to slits. 'I would say we were both at fault. I've no doubt, however, that you'd feel just as responsible if it were I who was hurt.'

Blythe's fine brows lifted. 'You think so?'

'Unless I've misjudged you.'

She smiled insincerely. 'It wouldn't worry me, Mr Daggart, if you'd broken both your legs.'

He was silent for a moment, and she thought he might go now he knew how she felt about him. But the next second he had straddled a chair and was facing her. 'Blythe, I was hoping our first meeting after all these years would turn out a little better than it did. Our colliding was nothing more than an unfortunate accident. You're surely not going to hold it against me?'

'Do you really think that if it wasn't for the accident I'd say yes?' she asked scornfully. 'Are you of the opinion that the way you treated me eleven years ago doesn't count?'

He studied her carefully for a second or two, and Blythe felt herself warming beneath his narrowed gaze. It was disconcerting not being able to see his eyes properly. She wondered whether it was deliberate. 'I don't recall treating you badly,' he said.

'Of course, you wouldn't remember, would you?' she thrust scathingly. 'You've no idea how I felt when you suddenly decided you didn't want to see me any more. No explanation, nothing. Just a sudden, abrupt end to our relationship.'

'Blythe, I——'

'No, don't bother to explain,' she said. 'I should have known you were only amusing yourself at my expense. How many other girls has it happened to? I wonder. I suppose I was what you would call one of your experiences. Men like you must have plenty.'

His eyes widened at her outburst. 'What a volatile lady you've turned into. I don't recall hearing you speak quite so vehemently before. You should have gone into the world of business, Blythe, you'd have done very well.'

'I may just do that,' she said.

He froze for an instant. 'You mean you're going to carry on with the business? You've made up your mind?'

'Not entirely.'

He frowned. 'What's making you hesitate?'

She put her head to one side and looked at him with deliberate insolence. 'There are things I have to look into.'

'Finances?'

'No.'

His frown deepened.

Blythe smiled. 'Don't worry your head about it. You'll find out in good time.'

'I don't know what you're talking about,' he said irritably.

Blythe wasn't sure whether she did either. But it would do him good to stew for a few days. 'Never mind, Coburn. And I'd like you to go now. I want an early night.'

He hauled himself to his feet with obvious reluctance. 'You won't accept my offer?'

'No. But thank you all the same.'

'Betty Rees will come round often?'

'If I know Betty, yes, she'll be here quite a lot.'

He pulled a card out of his pocket and put it down on the table. 'If you should ever need me, here's my number. You can ring me day or night.'

'How very kind of you.'

His lips thinned at the mockery in her tone. 'I'm quite sincere, Blythe. As you know, the Reeses aren't on the phone. What will you do if you feel worse?'

'I'll ring the doctor.'

He drummed his fingers angrily on the back of the chair, then he swung away. 'Goodnight, Blythe.' At the door, he turned. 'It might be a good idea if you give me your car keys. I'll get it repaired while you're out of action.'

And it would give him an excuse to call and see her again! She glared. 'It's all right. Ben will see to it.'

His nostrils flared. 'Blythe, Ben's not getting any younger. It's a five-mile walk back from the garage.'

She realised she was being ungracious. 'Very well. The keys are hanging up in the kitchen.'

In bed that night, Blythe decided Coburn Daggart was intruding into her personal life far more than she wanted him to. He had no business sending for the doctor, and she ought to have protested more strongly. Nor should she have let him take her car. She was inviting trouble.

Blythe lay awake a long time thinking about him. She even dreamt about him. And when she awoke he was in her thoughts. Abruptly she sat up. She would take a shower—she would wash that man right out of her hair, as the song went. But the sudden movement set off the pain in her head and she remembered Betty's orders. With a sigh, she lay down again.

It was another hour before the older woman arrived, calling cheerfully up the stairs, then busying herself cooking Blythe's breakfast, which she brought to her on a tray.

'How are you this morning?' Betty enquired briskly, plumping the pillows behind the girl before setting the tray across her lap. 'I've made you some nice scrambled egg and a slice of toast, and if you want any more you just ask.'

Blythe smiled. 'You're spoiling me. I don't feel there's anything wrong—only if I move quickly.'

'Of course, that's why the doctor told you to rest.'

'I can't sit and do nothing all day and every day. It will drive me crazy.'

'Nonsense. I'll set your lounger out in the garden and you can soak up the sun. Make the most of it while it's here.'

But a few hours being idle was more than Blythe could stand. In the end she went up to her father's bedroom and took out of his bureau the neat pile of diaries she had spotted yesterday. It was a wild hope that they might give her some clue as to why he had refused to sell to Coburn Daggart.

She had not known her father even kept a diary, yet here they all were, dating right back to the time he met her mother. He had poured his soul out on these pages. She could not read them, not the early ones. It seemed like an invasion of his privacy. Besides, they wouldn't tell her anything about Coburn. He hadn't bought Druid's then.

The year she was Wassail Queen, that was the one she wanted. Here it was. And here was the entry for that day. *My precious Blythe, how beautiful she looked. How very much like her mother. I wish she was here to see her.*

Blythe smiled to herself as she read on, but then a few pages later her smile changed to a frown. *Blythe's dating*

Daggart. Oh, lord. I'm going to have to send her away. I couldn't bear for it to happen all over again.

Blythe could not understand what he was saying. And then, later still, *My baby has left home today. God forgive me for sending her away, but it's for the best.*

That was when she had started art college. It had been her father's idea, but surely not deliberately to separate her from Daggart? She found that hard to believe. Besides, she had already finished with him and was glad to go—although her father hadn't known. Her pride had forbade her say anything.

Rapidly now Blythe flicked over the pages, searching for further clues. Another eighteen months went by, then: *Daggart came to see me today. He wants my land. I'll never sell, not to him, not to any member of the Foxley-Daggarts.*

Foxley-Daggart! *Foxley?* The Foxleys had owned Druid's Cider before Coburn Daggart bought it. Blythe hadn't known their full name was Foxley-Daggart. They had always been known as the Foxleys. And she thought they had all died.

A few days later. *Coburn Daggart made another offer. He must want the land badly. But no son of Drummond Foxley-Daggart will ever get his hands on anything of mine.*

By this time Blythe's head was spinning and aching so badly that she closed the diary and sat back in the chair. Coburn was Drummond Foxley's son! What a turn up for the books. She had been unaware there was a son. Obviously there had been much more going on at Druid's Cottage than she had ever imagined.

She still had not learned why her father hadn't wanted her to go out with Coburn, but it did give some sort of explanation as to why he had insisted she move to London. She had wondered at his change of heart, because when she'd suggested art college some months earlier he had been dead set against it.

And when Kate died in a car accident some years later he wouldn't even let her come home then. She had begun a job in London and he had insisted she stay because he knew how happy she was.

How sad he must have been. How sad and lonely. And yet he had covered it all up because he didn't want her to associate with Coburn Daggart. Would the diary tell her why?

Later she would read more, tomorrow maybe. Her head was throbbing intolerably.

When Betty came at lunch time the pain had not eased, and she was so pale the woman sent her to bed. It was early evening when she awoke, and there was a note propped on her bedside table. 'Blythe, I brought your dinner but you were still asleep. I'll come back again around eight. Don't you dare get out of bed. Betty.'

Blythe smiled to herself and lay there feeling warm and comfortable. Her head was much better and her thoughts naturally turned to her father's diaries. They were tucked away in the drawer of her dressing-table now. She was tempted to fetch them and read on, but at that moment Betty arrived.

She fussed around Blythe like a mother hen, asking her over and over again how she felt, sitting her up and plumping her pillows and finally putting a delicious roast lamb dinner in front of her.

'You really shouldn't go to so much trouble,' said Blythe, feeling guilty because she wasn't really ill. She could have looked after herself, she was sure.

'What trouble?' demanded Betty. 'I have to cook for me and Ben, don't I? It's no trouble to cook for one more. I used to bring your father the odd dinner as well. He was very grateful.'

'I've been reading his diaries,' admitted Blythe.

'So that's what caused your headache,' said Betty accusingly. 'The doctor told Ben you weren't to do anything, and I'm sure that includes reading. Your father's handwriting's not easy to decipher at the best of times. I want you to promise me, Blythe, that you won't read any more until the doctor gives you the all-clear.'

Reluctantly Blythe agreed. 'Do you know anything about the Foxleys, who used to own Druid's Cider?'

Betty frowned. 'Now, what makes you ask about them?'

'Something my father wrote.'

'Mmm, they were here a long time, I know that much. Generations of them. They were not a family who were very much liked, I'm afraid. From what I've heard there was gypsy blood in them. It's amazing they ever settled. But I'm sure you don't want to go bothering your pretty head about them. They're past history.'

'Why was Druid's Cider sold? What happened, did the family die out?'

Betty lifted her ample shoulders. 'I believe so. There was a son, but he never lived here. I don't know what happened to him.'

'My father wrote something about the Foxley-Daggarts,' said Blythe softly, closely watching the other woman's reaction.

'Foxley-Daggart? Was that their name? I never knew. They were always called Foxleys for as far back as I can remember. Daggart, you say?' Then her eyes widened. 'Daggart? You don't think that——? No! He couldn't be.'

'Why not? It makes sense.'

Betty's frown deepened. 'The son? He came back! We all thought he'd bought Druid's Cider, but maybe he inherited it instead? And he's made it bigger and better than ever it was. What a turn up for the books.'

'Why didn't my father like him?'

'I think we've talked enough about the Foxley-Daggarts.' Betty's face suddenly set. 'Finish your dinner. I'll go and tidy up downstairs.'

It was an excuse, and Blythe knew it. The house was already like a show-place. Betty knew something and she didn't want to say. Blythe chewed her meat thoughtfully. Maybe the diaries would tell her? But she would have to curb her curiosity and wait until the rotten pain had gone out of her head.

Blythe was in a lather of impatience during the next couple of days. Betty clucked and fussed and wouldn't let her do anything, not even read a paper. 'I'm sure Dr Fullerton didn't mean you to be this strict,' grumbled Blythe.

'And I'm sure if he knew how bad you were when I came the other day he'd be in full agreement.'

On the third day of her enforced rest, Coburn came to see her. Betty let him in with the strict injunction that he was to stay no longer than half an hour.

He wore denim today, jeans, and a sleeveless jacket over a red T-shirt. Designer jeans, of course, and despite his casual appearance he still looked very much the man who had everything.

Blythe looked up from the couch where Betty insisted she spend most of her time. There was no welcoming smile on her face, even though her pulses leapt a little.

He came straight across, and to her astonishment dropped a casual kiss on her brow. 'How's the invalid today?'

'Getting better,' she said quietly, fighting the sudden prickling of her senses.

'I hear you had a relapse?'

Blythe frowned. 'I don't think so.'

'Betty said she came and found you looking like a ghost, and you complained your head was throbbing fit to burst. You should have sent for the doctor again.'

'I'd been reading, that's all. I'm all right now.' She wished Betty hadn't told him.

'You still look very pale.'

'Because I've been sitting indoors.' The blue skies had been replaced by threatening thunderclouds. They had had a few bursts of rain and the occasional sunny period, but it certainly wasn't outdoor weather.

He pulled up a chair and sat close to her. 'Your car will be ready tomorrow. I've arranged to have it delivered. But you're not to use it yet, do you hear?'

'You're as bad as Betty,' she complained.

'Doctor's orders.'

'I'm not so sure.' His eyes were more blue than grey today, unless it was a reflection from his jacket. And his straw-coloured hair was for once tamed. It was straight, except where it curled above his collar, swept back to reveal a noble forehead. She wondered whether all the Foxley-Daggarts had had blond hair? And she wondered whether she dared ask him if he was one of them?

'Something tells me you're not taking too kindly to your enforced rest?'

'No, I'm not,' she replied with feeling. 'Betty won't even let me read, or watch television for more than a few minutes. I listen to the radio and play some of my father's tapes, and get totally bored.'

'And it's all my fault?' he grinned. 'Is that what you're saying?'

'Something like that.'

'Perhaps I could make it up to you?'

Blythe's fine brows lifted. 'I doubt it.'

'I thought I might come and pick you up in the morning and take you out for the day.'

'No, thanks.'

'You wouldn't have to do anything. Just sit in my car and look pretty. A change of scenery can be a wonderful tonic.'

His eyes were on her face and Blythe found it difficult to look away. 'Why are you bothering?'

'Does there have to be a reason?'

'Where you're concerned, yes. Are you still trying to work on me? Still hoping I'll come up with the right response?'

Fractionally his eyes hardened, scarcely enough for her to notice, but she did. 'I'm prepared to wait until you've made up your mind,' he said. 'I'm not hurrying you. This has nothing at all to do with it. I thought you deserved a break.'

'How kind,' she mocked.

'I'm sincere, Blythe. Give me one good reason why you can't come.'

She lifted her shoulders expressively. 'You know I don't have one.'

'Then it's settled?'

It occurred to Blythe that, if she did agree to go out with him, she might be able to find out something about his family. It was all the incentive she needed. A smile broke out on her face. 'Yes, it's a date.'

'Good.' His grin was even wider than hers. 'You won't regret it, I know. I'll get my housekeeper to pack us a picnic lunch, and I know a perfect little cove where we won't be disturbed.'

Blythe frowned. 'I'm not worried about other people,' she said at once.

'But I am.'

'Why?'

'Does a man need a reason to keep a beautiful girl to himself?'

Blythe tossed an impatient head at his flattery, then winced at the pain. She was still far from well, even though she was reluctant to admit it, even to herself.

'Perhaps you'd like to choose where we go?'

'It doesn't really matter,' she said with pretended indifference. But somehow the thought of being alone with him for a whole day, completely alone, sent a shiver down her spine. Apprehension or excitement? Fear or anticipation? Blythe wasn't sure which.

He called for her at ten, and he wore his black cords and a white T-shirt. He looked very muscular and magnificent, and they drove in silence for the first few miles. Not an uncomfortable silence, discovered Blythe in surprise. She felt relaxed with him, and this was amazing considering the depth of her hostility.

Actually her mind was full of the questions she wanted to ask. She had read no more of her father's diaries, and there was so much she still knew nothing about. She hoped Coburn would be able to provide some answers.

The sun had come out again this morning and it was a perfect day for a picnic. 'What are you thinking?' Coburn's voice suddenly broke into her thoughts.

Blythe gave a tiny smile. 'You're not going to believe this, but I was thinking how comfortable I feel with you.'

'I'm pleased,' he said, and he looked it. His eyes crinkled at the corners and he touched her hand briefly. 'It's the first time you've relaxed with me since we met up again.'

'You must admit they were rather extenuating circumstances. I was very angry.'

'And rightly so. I should never have swung into your drive so recklessly.'

'You're sending me up now,' she accused.

'Would I do that?' He caught her hand and raised it to his lips in a gallant gesture that set the adrenalin pounding through Blythe's veins. But she must remember that there was a purpose behind today. This was not a pleasure trip. She needed to find out why her father had been so against this man and his family.

They were silent again as he drove towards the coast, and Blythe would have missed the narrow lane he turned into, its entrance almost hidden by two giant oaks. There was no sign to say where it led, and it got narrower and narrower until it was nothing more than a rutted track.

Then, suddenly, there was the beach in front of them. The tiniest, loveliest little bay she had ever seen. A pocket handkerchief of coarse sand, rocks tumbling over themselves, cliffs rising on either side. And the sea was an impossible blue—impossible for England, anyway. It was perfect.

She turned and smiled involuntarily into Coburn's face. 'It's lovely. How did you ever find it?' And without waiting for him to answer she scrambled out of the car and ran forward on to the sand, kicking off her shoes and dancing around like a child. She wore a simple cotton dress and looked no older than the sixteen years she had been when she first met him.

'Blythe, I think you ought to take things easy.' He was at her side, a restraining hand on her shoulder.

She whirled to face him. 'Why? It's wonderful, I love it. And I feel as fit as a fiddle.'

Their eyes met and held, and yet again Blythe was unprepared when he gathered her to him and kissed her.

CHAPTER THREE

BLYTHE struggled like a wildcat to free herself from Coburn's embrace, but his hold on her was invincible. 'Coburn, no,' she protested strongly against his mouth.

'You never used to object,' he muttered, running the tip of his tongue erotically over her lips.

'Things were different then,' she claimed, trying to ignore the sensations his touch ignited. 'I thought that——' She tailed off. How could she say that in those days she had thought their relationship would last? How naïve he would think her.

'Yes, things were different,' he confirmed. 'Very different. But now you're a grown woman and, if I may say so, far more desirable. Not that you weren't a pretty little thing then.'

Yet he had dropped her with no word of explanation. She would never forgive him for that. Blythe renewed her struggles, but Coburn was not ready to let her go.

He kissed her again and all her self-control vanished. Her heart beat as though it had gone crazy, and desire flooded her loins, far more intense than it had ever been in the past. She had the insane wish that this moment could go on forever.

She parted her lips to accept his deepening kiss, her arms winding round his neck of their own volition. The years had not lessened the effect he had on her.

When he finally put her from him, Blythe was the one to feel disappointed. 'I think that's enough for now,' he said, but the promise in his eyes sent fresh shivers of anticipation through her limbs.

The picnic lunch was an unqualified success. His housekeeper had packed huge Cornish pasties, kept warm in a special thermal container. Fresh rolls and salad. Stilton and fruit and biscuits. A chilled fruit punch as well as a thermos of coffee. It was all delicious and appetising, and all the nicer for being eaten out of doors.

Blythe licked her fingers and wiped them on her napkin. 'That was lovely. Thank you very much.'

'The pleasure is mine in seeing you enjoy yourself,' he said. 'How are you feeling, Blythe? You're not overdoing it?'

'I'm fine,' she replied, smiling warmly, wondering if he felt the same heady happiness. She must be careful, or she would forget the real reason she had agreed to come out with him. It was ridiculous really, allowing him to get through to her like this, but Coburn was not the sort of man you could ignore, especially when he set himself out to please.

'No headache?'

'Only the tiniest little one.'

He packed their plates into the hamper and moved it off the blanket they had spread on the ground. 'Lie down.'

'And you?'

He smiled. 'I'll take a walk, then I'll join you.'

'Can't I walk too?' Her eyes were wide and pleading. 'I'm very full. I'm sure it would be bad for my indigestion if I lay down so soon after eating.'

In response he held out his hand. 'Do you always get your own way?'

'Most of the time,' she confessed as they began walking.

'I imagine your father spoilt you. Are you an only child?'

Blythe nodded, then wished she hadn't as a sharp pain reminded her that she still had a long way to go before she was fully recovered. 'My mother died when I was only three. She picked up some mysterious bug and never recovered.'

He grimaced sympathetically. 'You don't remember her, then?'

'No. I have a vague image of someone who always smelled nice, someone who gave me lots of love, but that's about all. My father used to talk about her sometimes, but never in front of Kate.'

'So Kate was your stepmother?' A tiny frown creased the space between his eyes. 'I never realised that.'

'I think my father only married her for my sake.' Blythe bent down and picked up a pebble worn smooth by the constant pounding of the ocean. 'He was very upset when my mother died. I don't think he ever really got over it. He kept all the love-letters she sent him. Don't you find that surprising?'

His brows lifted. 'Indeed I do. The few times I met your father, he struck me as being as hard as nails.'

'That's because you only saw the business side of him.' Blythe tossed the pebble from hand to hand, weighing up what she was going to say next. 'Is it true that you tried to buy him out, the same as you're doing me?'

A muscle jerked in Coburn's jaw. 'Who told you that?' And the tone of his voice subtly altered.

Blythe stopped walking and faced him. 'Never mind who told me, is it true?'

'Yes, I asked him,' he answered, and Blythe thought she heard a defensive note in his voice.

'And he refused?'

'Every time. He didn't seem to like me, Blythe, and yet I'm quite sure I never did anything to upset him.'

'Except take me out,' she said quietly.

A frown slashed his brow. 'You don't think it was because I'd touched his precious little daughter? Was that it? Is that what you're trying to tell me?' He sounded incredulous.

'I don't know,' she said. 'It's the only thing I can think of.'

Her father had sent her away because she'd got friendly with Coburn. It was nonsense, and yet that was what he had implied. *I don't want it to happen all over again.* He didn't want what to happen, for heaven's sake? And quite clearly Coburn didn't have the answer either. It had been a waste of time coming out with him today.

'Was it your father's idea that you went to art college in London?'

Blythe shrugged, not wishing to incriminate her father in this way. 'I'd always wanted to go.'

'But it was very sudden, wasn't it? You never said anything to me.'

Blythe smashed the pebble down. 'So what? I didn't have to tell you everything, did I?'

'You were very young to be let loose in London on your own. He really must have had it in for me. I wonder why?'

'You're as wise as me,' snapped Blythe. 'Shall we sit down? I'm suddenly very tired.'

'Of course.' He put his hand on her elbow and led her back to the blanket, making sure she was comfortable before sitting himself. He rested back on the heels of his hands and stared far out to sea.

The sun turned his hair to burnished gold, his profile was definitely autocratic. He could not possibly be descended from a gypsy. He had a high forehead and a fine straight nose, and Blythe could see a whispering of blond hairs down his arms.

She was strongly tempted to touch him, despite everything. Despite the harsh words recently uttered. Despite the way he had hurt her all those years ago. Despite the accident, when he had virtually accused her of being at fault. There was a hungering inside her to be held in his arms, a need for him. Nothing had really altered. She still felt the same yearning deep down inside as she had when she was sixteen and he was her first love.

There were two sides to Coburn's nature. One when he was hard and impossible. This was the new Coburn. There had been times in the past when he'd had too high an opinion of himself, but he had always been likeable. Now he could hurt her with words or a single glance.

Yet in another instance he could be kind and compassionate and attentive, loving even. But was he like this for a reason? Was he deliberately soft-soaping her because he wanted to buy her out? And was she reacting in exactly the way he anticipated?

The thought sent a ripple of shock-waves through her body, and she closed her eyes tightly.

'Blythe, what's wrong?'

She had not realised he was watching her.

'Are you in pain?'

'A little,' she agreed, and now she thought about it her head had begun to ache again. It occurred to her that it always did when she felt stressed.

He groaned softly. 'I knew you'd done too much. It's my fault. I'm sorry.' He stroked her brow, his fingertips gentle and soothing. He had a beautiful touch, seeming to know exactly where it hurt most. 'Do you forgive me, Blythe?'

She gave a tiny helpless smile. He had a way with him when he was trying to curry favour that she found impossible to resist. 'It's not your fault.'

He continued to massage her temples and her nape beneath her hair until Blythe relaxed so much that she fell asleep. When she awoke he was watching her, an intensely thoughtful expression on his face, which changed instantly to a smile when she opened her eyes. He ran a finger down the length of her nose. 'Better?' And he touched her cheek, letting his hand remain there to assure her of his concern.

'Much better,' she agreed, pushing herself into a sitting position.

He cupped her chin and smiled into her eyes. He dropped a kiss on her brow and then sat away from her. 'I think I ought to take you home.'

Blythe could not make up her mind about him. If he was trying to get round her, then he was a brilliant actor and psychologist. He was saying and doing all the right things. Maybe she ought not to be suspicious. Maybe he was genuine. She had no real way of knowing. Only time would tell.

They had a silent and comfortable journey home, and he did not suggest coming into the house. 'I'll see you tomorrow,' he said instead.

Blythe's eyes widened. 'You're not taking another day off?'

'And set a bad example to my staff?' he asked sternly. 'Miss Berensen, how could you think such a thing?' Then he grinned. 'I thought we might have dinner together tomorrow night? I'll pick you up and we'll go back to my place and——' He trailed off at her sudden resolute expression. 'No?'

'I don't think so,' she said. 'Thank you for the offer, but——'

'You've seen enough of me for a while? OK.' He accepted her refusal when she had expected him to argue. 'I won't push you. We'll make it Friday. No, let's leave it till the weekend. Saturday night and——' his brows rose questioningly '—Sunday morning?'

Blythe shook her head, but could not help smiling. 'Saturday night.'

He shrugged easily. 'You can't blame a guy for trying.'

Blythe was grinning to herself when she went into the house. How could she not like him? She could not deny that today had been a lot of fun, even if she had not exactly achieved her object.

Betty was hovering anxiously in the kitchen. She had not been pleased when Blythe had told her she was going out. Now she pulled out a chair and insisted the girl sit down. 'I was about to pop a pie in the oven for your supper. You look tired, my dear. Do you think it was wise going out so soon?'

'Betty, don't fuss so,' she protested, with a reassuring smile. 'I've had a wonderful time. If I'd stayed in any longer I'd have gone crazy. You're right, though, I am a bit tired now.'

The woman tutted as she filled the kettle and made a pot of tea. 'You're not thinking of doing it again?'

'Not until Saturday. Coburn's invited me up to his house for dinner.'

Betty pursed her lips. 'You seem to be getting mighty friendly with him all of a sudden. Your father wouldn't have liked it.'

'Coburn's quite nice when you get to know him.' Blythe surprised herself by sticking up for him.

'Hmph!' snorted Betty. 'If he's anything like his—like the rest of his family, then you'd best stay away from him.'

Blythe frowned. 'What are you saying, Betty?'

'Nothing.' The woman clammed up.

'You said the other day that no one liked the Foxleys. Why was that?'

'Nothing you need concern your pretty head about. Drink your tea.'

It was clear she was not going to say anything else, already regretting those few hastily spoken words.

Blythe puzzled about them for the rest of the day. Tomorrow, when she was rested, she would carry on reading her father's diaries. It was the only way she was going to find anything out.

The next morning Coburn phoned her early. 'Good morning, my beautiful Blythe. How are you today?'

'You've got me out of bed,' she accused, but her tone was light and a delicious tremor ran through her limbs.

'Have I? Should I say I'm sorry? But I wanted to speak to you before I left, so I'm not really. You haven't answered my question.'

She smiled. 'I'm feeling pretty good at this moment.'

'Me, too,' he said in a low growl. 'What are you wearing? No, don't tell me, let me guess. A winceyette nightie that comes right down to your toes.'

'How clever of you,' she mocked, looking at her pretty shortie nightdress. 'It has pink rosebuds on it and used to belong to my grandmother.'

'I bet she didn't look half as pretty as you.'

'Of course not.'

'I can't wait until Saturday, Blythe.' There was a deep hunger in his voice which sounded genuine enough.

'I'm afraid you'll have to.'

'You're not going to change your mind and let me see you earlier?'

'No.'

'A pity. And I must go now. Climb back into your bed, my lovely, and think of me.'

He had made sure of that. She tingled from top to toe, and there was an inane grin on her face as she slid between the sheets. She had to be wrong about him. No man would behave as he did purely to clinch a deal. Would he?

Blythe did not stay in bed long. She was down in the kitchen making toast when Betty arrived. 'Don't shout at me,' she said to the woman at once. 'I'm feeling much better, honestly.'

'I must admit you do look it,' admitted Mrs Rees with obvious reluctance.

'And I think I can manage by myself now.'

Betty eyed her suspiciously.

'It's putting you to so much trouble when you have your own house and Ben to look after.'

'Ben can look after himself,' came Betty's caustic reply. 'It's no bother, I assure you. Now, what are you going to have with that toast? Bacon and tomatoes or poached egg?'

Blythe settled for the bacon, and somehow managed to persuade Betty that she needn't come back later in the day. 'If you really want to, you can come again in the morning.'

'Very well,' said the woman unwillingly. 'But I'll tell Ben to pop in if he's passing. Just in case there's anything you need. By the way, your car was delivered yesterday while you were out. They've made a good job of it. I hope that man Daggart's paying?'

'He is,' confirmed Blythe strongly. No matter how friendly they became, this was something she had no intention of changing her mind about.

As soon as she had the house to herself, Blythe went upstairs and reached for her father's diaries, settling down in her bedroom chair, planning to spend the next few hours reading steadily through them.

But it did not work out quite like that. The phone rang and it was Megan. She had a day off and was lonely, she complained, and spent over an hour filling Blythe in on everything that had happened since she'd left. 'Bruce is like a bear with a sore head. I didn't realise he felt that way about you.'

'I wish he didn't,' admitted Blythe. 'I like him, but that's all.'

'I keep trying to fix him up, but to no avail,' grumbled Megan. 'Which brings me to the real reason I'm phoning. There's this girl who's come to work at our place. She's a beauty, and I'm sure he'll like her. She has nowhere to stay, and I was wondering whether she could have your room—until she gets fixed up—unless of course you're planning on coming back soon?'

Blythe had promised to let Megan know as soon as possible what she intended doing. She was actually paying the other girl half the rent just to keep the room for her. Now she was being faced with an ultimatum.

If she let this girl have her room, she would have nowhere to live when she did go back. It would be the devil's own job getting the girl out. It was like that in bedsit land.

But was she going to sell her father's business? Or was she going to dig her heels in and consistently refuse all Coburn's offers, no matter how nice he was to her? Was she going to try and pull the business back together for her father's sake? He must have had some very good reason for refusing to sell—if she could only find out what it was.

'Blythe—are you still there?' Megan's anxious voice broke into her thoughts.

'Yes, yes, of course I am. I was thinking. I actually don't know what I'm doing yet, Megan. Things aren't what I expected.'

'Then Sophie can stay for a while?'

'So long as I can still have the room if I need it?'

'Of course, Blythe. It's my house and you're my friend. I'd never see you out on the street. Thanks for being so understanding. And as I say, it might get Bruce off your back. I believe he phoned you the other day?'

'That's right. He's talking about coming here for his holidays.'

'I'll try to dissuade him,' said Megan. 'Or let Sophie do it for me. 'Bye for now, Blythe. Keep in touch.'

No sooner had Blythe put down the phone than it rang again, and then Ben popped in, and the whole day seemed to pass without her getting a chance to read the diaries.

Friday followed a similar pattern, with both Betty and Ben calling in to see her, and various phone calls that were both time-consuming and tedious.

On Saturday she went out shopping and on an impulse bought a new dress. Not that she wanted to impress Coburn tonight, she told herself firmly, but she hadn't had anything new in ages. She deserved a treat.

The dress was pink and dove-grey, in a soft, swirly material that flattered and clung. She opened the door when Coburn arrived and he took one look at her and said, 'I can see tonight is going to be a night to remember.'

Blythe felt a moment of doubt. She hoped she had not created the wrong impression. Perhaps she ought not to have given in to the moment of madness that had made her buy the dress?

She had fixed her hair on top of her head in a cluster of curls, soft tendrils hiding the fading bruise and framing her face. Make-up she had kept to a minimum: shiny blue eyeshadow to emphasise the blue of her eyes, mascara to thicken her lashes, and a touch of rose-pink lipstick.

Crystal pendant ear-rings completed the picture. They were her mother's, her real mother, and she treasured them so much. Her father had given them to her on her twenty-first birthday. 'I know Pamela would want you to have them,' he had said, and she'd thought there was a shimmer of tears in his eyes. They weren't the only pieces of jewellery she owned of Pamela's, but they were her favourite.

As Coburn took her arm and led her out to his car, Blythe felt tingles of awareness run like quicksilver through her veins. It occurred to her that, no matter how much she hated or distrusted him, there would always be this element of sexual awareness. The feeling had been there right from the start, from the second their eyes met at the wassailing, and she knew that he felt it too. But that was all it was, a physical need, nothing more, and she would be as well to remember it. It would be so easy to make a fool of herself for a second time.

Coburn was not in the Ferrari tonight. A navy blue BMW saloon stood sedately in front of the house. It was much easier to climb into, but she guessed just as powerful under the bonnet. Coburn wouldn't settle for anything less. He was the type of person who conducted his life in top gear.

The picnic on the beach had actually surprised her. She thought crowded places and a lively atmosphere more his scene. He wasn't a romantic. It made her wonder all over again whether this caring almost protective image wasn't simply part of a devious scheme.

She slid on to the grey leather seat, sinking into it, feeling the luxury as well as smelling it. Coburn closed the door, after carefully making sure the folds of her dress were out of the way. The brief touch of his hand against her thigh sent Blythe's senses spinning, and she chided herself for reacting so violently to what was no more than accidental contact.

By the time he had walked round to his side of the car she had steadied herself, and when he got in she was looking in wonderment at the complicated dashboard. 'Do you need a degree to drive this thing?'

He grinned. 'It's a wonderful machine. Fully computerised. It knows everything that's going on. Coupled with 115 brake horsepower, ellipsoid headlights—more light, no dazzle—and something else that might interest you—regenerating bumpers. Which means,' he went on when she frowned, 'they can take a knock and bounce back into place. Not a heavy knock, mind, but say you met another car as you were gently pulling out of your drive, then——'

She aimed a blow at him, but he caught her hand and pressed her palm to his mouth. 'I'm glad you agreed to have dinner with me. I've been looking forward to it for days.'

And, in truth, so had Blythe.

'My housekeeper's prepared a gourmet meal. I trust you can do it justice? She'll be mortally offended if you don't.'

'I'll do my best,' replied Blythe demurely. This evening was going to be more difficult than she had imagined. Coburn was determined to make everything perfect, and she was not certain that she trusted his motives.

Blythe had never seen Coburn's house. She had heard it was impressive, but nothing had prepared her for the spectacle that met her eyes.

The drive first of all took them through an area of woodland. It was cool and green and gracefully beautiful, but Blythe imagined that in winter it might be dark and forbidding, the skeletal branches of the trees twisting themselves into eerie, frightening shapes.

Suddenly the trees on one side of the road gave way to velvet-smooth lawns, dotted here and there with easy to maintain conifer and heather beds. They passed over a tiny hump-backed bridge, beneath which burbled a fresh-water stream, and here was the house. A yellow-painted, thatched-roof building that looked enormous.

'My humble cottage,' he announced proudly.

'Some cottage!'

He grinned. 'It was once four tiny cottages belonging to estate workers. Druid's Cottages, they were called. It was knocked into one by my father. He had grandiose ideas. And now it's simply Druid's Cottage.'

'It looks beautiful.'

'I like it,' he said. 'I always knew I would come back here one day.'

The car came to a halt and he was out before Blythe could ask him about the split with his family. It had been an ideal opportunity and she had lost it. By the time he opened her door and gave her his hand, he had changed the subject. 'Come, let me show you around before we go inside.'

He was once again the enthusiastic boy, and it was infectious. Blythe smiled as he pulled her along, gasping when she saw the swimming pool and the purpose-built wooden building at the side of it that housed a sauna. Beyond as well was a tennis court and a putting green, and he dragged her from one to the other at the speed of light.

'You live here all by yourself?' she asked incredulously.

'Unless you'd care to share it with me,' he smiled.

Blythe knew her worst fears were realised. 'As your wife, of course,' she thrust sarcastically. 'So that my property would automatically become yours. My, you're devious.'

Abruptly the good humour left his face, the hard angles were back. 'You think I'd do a thing like that?'

'I'm certain of it,' she insisted, painfully unhappy all of a sudden, even though she had been half prepared for something like this to happen. Nothing so serious as a marriage proposal, though.

'May I ask what I've done to warrant such deep distrust?' His hard grey eyes were narrowed on her face, and Blythe felt tiny shivers of apprehension run down her spine. What had happened to that lovely warm feeling of a few seconds ago?

'I'll tell you what you've done,' she thrust bitterly. 'You made my father some ridiculously high offers for his property. Out of all proportion to its worth. And now that I'm refusing to sell as well, you're trying a different tactic. You really must be desperate. All I can say is, thank heaven I saw through you.'

He eyed her coldly. 'I suggest you think again about what I did say, Blythe. At no time did I mention marriage. It was you who jumped to that conclusion.'

Blythe frowned and recalled the conversation. Colour mounted her cheeks as she realised that he was right. He had merely suggested she might like to share the house with him. It was probably even a joke, as he had been smiling when he spoke. She felt mortified, but covered it up in anger. 'Of course you meant it. This is just your way of trying to make me look like a fool.'

His mouth compressed into a grim, straight line and his fists curled at his sides. Blythe got the impression that if she were a man he would take a punch at her. 'Who told you about my offers?' he asked abruptly.

She was glad he had changed the subject. 'My solicitor.'

'Alan Ridsdale?'

'Yes.'

'He and your father were buddies,' he said pointedly.
'It was probably he who advised your father not to sell.
Though heaven knows why. And now I suppose he's
telling you not to sell?'

'It wasn't Alan who encouraged my father.'

Coburn looked at her sharply. 'What makes you say
that? Solicitors are sly old devils. He probably told your
father to hold out for as much as he could get. Well, a
man has his limits, and I'd reached mine when your
father died.'

'Did he know that?'

'How the hell do I know? And what makes you so
sure it wasn't Ridsdale's doing?'

'I just know, that's all,' Blythe mumbled, walking
away from him. She couldn't tell him about the entries
in her father's diary. They were too personal. But she
did need to find out what it was her father had against
Drummond Foxley-Daggart. She mustn't fall out with
Coburn, not yet. Not until the mystery was solved.

She turned again abruptly. 'Coburn, I'm sorry. I spoke
out of turn. Let's not spoil the evening.'

He eyed her brutally. 'I think the evening's already
spoilt. But Smitty will never forgive us if we don't eat
the meal she's spent hours preparing.'

Blythe followed him into the house, still deeply em-
barrassed by her *faux pas*. His housekeeper was a smart,
slender woman with an air about her that suggested she
would be happier being mistress of the house, instead
of looking after it for someone else. She was probably
in her early sixties and, judging by her ringless fingers,
had never married.

Smitty looked long and hard at Blythe after the in-
troductions were made, as if assessing whether she was
good enough for Coburn. Blythe wondered what he had
told the woman about her. But, whatever it was, Smitty

merely nodded a greeting and disappeared into the depths of the house.

'Do you entertain often?' Blythe questioned in an attempt to get the conversation flowing again.

'If you're asking whether I bring girlfriends home, the answer's no. But I have been known to throw the odd party.' He smiled humourlessly. 'Quite riotous occasions they've turned out, too. Smitty doesn't approve.'

'How long has she been with you?'

'Goodness knows. She was here in my father's time.'

Blythe stored the information away. Smitty could prove useful—if she ever unbent sufficiently to talk.

'What happened—between you and your father?' she asked next, following him into what was obviously a much-used sitting-room. It had an oak-beamed ceiling and white walls, red carpet and curtains, and a chintzy sofa and chairs in red and brown. It was a cosy room. Blythe liked it.

'You know about the rift?'

'Not really,' admitted Blythe. 'I've heard snippets of information and put two and two together——'

'And probably made five,' he said tersely. 'What would you like to drink?'

'A dry martini, please.'

There was silence while he mixed her martini and poured himself a Scotch. What had promised to be an enjoyable evening had been spoilt by her crazy mistake. Blythe sat down on the sofa and watched him.

He wore smart black trousers this evening and a black shirt with white collar and cuffs, and the black leather boots. He looked masculine and sexy, and Blythe stupidly hoped that he wouldn't be angry with her for long.

He handed her her drink and dropped down into one of the armchairs, leaning back, resting an ankle on the other knee. 'What makes you so interested in my family?'

Blythe was disappointed he had not sat by her. She took a sip of her martini. 'I only discovered the other day that you were actually Drummond Foxley's son.'

'And how did you find that out? Village gossip?'

'No, I saw the name Foxley-Daggart in something my father had written and it suddenly all dropped into place.'

'So—now you know. This place, the cider works, they're all mine by rights.'

'Did your father want you to have them?'

'The hell he did. He turned me and my mother out.'

His abrupt disclosure shocked Blythe. 'I didn't know that. Why? What had you done?'

'Done?' His blond brows rose. 'I'd done nothing. I was a mere child. But according to my father I was a nuisance, a hindrance. I was about twelve or thirteen, intensely curious, and he couldn't conduct his affairs with me around.'

'Affairs?'

'That's right. Surely you knew that? He was notorious for his fast living. My mother used to turn a blind eye, more fool her, until one day he met another woman whom he claimed he actually wanted to marry. So out went my mother, and me with her. They were divorced and I never saw him again.'

'Did he marry this woman?'

'Not so far as I know. I believe she died before his divorce came through.'

Blythe could feel no pity. It sounded to her as though Drummond Foxley-Daggart had got what was coming to him.

'Is that why you dropped the name Foxley?'

'That's right. I didn't want to associate myself with him.'

'Is your mother still alive?'

He nodded. 'She's living in America now. She married again and is very happy.'

'And how did you come to own this house and the business if your father didn't want you to have it?'

Coburn snorted derisively. 'By some lack of insight he never changed his will, so my mother got the lot. And promptly gave it to me. She didn't want to set foot inside this house again. It held too many bad memories.' He paused. 'And now you know all about me.' Then finished his drink in one swallow. 'Shall we go in to dinner?'

Blythe was quietly thoughtful as she followed Coburn into the dining-room. He had told her much more than she'd expected, and yet it still did not clarify the entry in her father's diary. He had hated Drummond Foxley-Daggart with an intensity that was frightening, and he had sent her away so that she wouldn't associate with his son. But why? *Why?* Where would she find the answer?

The meal was superb. Thin slices of Parma ham served with iced melon to start with, veal cutlets in a creamed mushroom sauce, accompanied by sautéd potatoes, broccoli spears and French beans, followed by peaches soaked in syrup on a bed of strawberry mousse, topped by fresh strawberries and cream. Wickedly rich, but delicious.

They drank a whole bottle of wine between them, and by the time she had finished Blythe felt fit to burst. 'You weren't exaggerating when you said Smitty was a good cook. I shan't eat again for a week.'

He smiled at last. 'She certainly excels herself when I'm entertaining. When I'm here on my own it's a different story. Bangers and mash every day.'

'I don't believe that,' said Blythe, returning his smile. During dinner they had chatted desultorily, but had been unable to recapture their earlier rapport. He seemed really hurt by her accusation, though she couldn't be sure whether it was all an act.

They took their coffee into his sitting-room and he offered her a brandy, but she refused. The wine had already gone to her head. He lit up a cigar and watched her through the blue haze.

Blythe could not help asking the question that was uppermost in her mind. 'Why is owning my land so important to you?'

He shook his head, as if unable to understand the need for such a question. 'Isn't it obvious?'

'But Berry's Cider was there first,' she retorted. 'It's not my fault if you bought up all the land around.' There was a light of battle in her huge blue eyes.

'I want to make Druid's the biggest and best cider-makers in the country.'

'You could have a long wait,' she said, a stubborn set to her jaw, 'because until I find out why my father wouldn't sell to you, then I won't sell either.'

He eyed her grimly. 'So it's stalemate? In fact, you might never find out. I think it's time you went home

CHAPTER FOUR

BLYTHE hardly slept that night. Her head ached intolerably and she wished she had never accepted Coburn's dinner invitation. It had turned out nothing like she expected.

Jack, his gardener-cum-handyman-cum-chauffeur, had driven her home, and she had no idea when she was going to see Coburn again. By Sunday morning she was bad-tempered and tired, and could have fallen out with her own shadow.

She drank several cups of tea but ate nothing. It was another warm, sunny day, so she fetched her father's diaries and took them outside, determined to read right through them. Somehow she had to find out what had caused the friction between her father and Drummond Foxley.

But as she flicked through the pages there was nothing to tell her what she wanted to know. She read that Drummond Foxley-Daggart had died and her father felt deeply relieved. Then Coburn turned up on the scene, and he was worried it would start all over again. Her father, if no one else, knew that Coburn was Drummond's son. But what *it* was she had no idea.

When she put the diaries down it was almost lunch time. There had been reference to further offers by Coburn, but that was all, nothing about the friction between Drummond and himself.

Blythe made a ham sandwich, having no inclination to cook, and as she chewed it occurred to her that she was going about things the wrong way. It was the earlier diaries she should be reading, the ones she had cast to one side because of the heartbreaking references to her mother. They were back in her father's bureau now, but these, if any, would tell her about Drummond Foxley-Daggart.

After rinsing her plate and cup, Blythe rushed up to her father's room. The phone rang but she ignored it. She pulled up a chair to his desk and sat down. Her heart was beating quite quickly. Surely now she would find the answer?

January 1st. Six months before her mother died. *What a start to a new year. How am I going to live without Pamela? I never dreamt she would do this to me.*

Blythe frowned and turned the pages quickly. What did he mean? Was it the beginning of her illness? But he claimed she had done something to him! What?

There followed several blank days when her father had written nothing, which she found most strange. In all of the other diaries he had filled in something every day, even if it was only a reference to the weather.

January 13th. I'll kill Drummond Foxley-Daggart if I get the chance. What does Pamela see in him? She always swore to love me till the end of my days. I love her so very, very much. Please come back to me, Pamela. I can't live without you. If not for my sake, for Blythe's. Our precious baby's missing you, missing you——

Blythe sat transfixed, suddenly ice-cold, her skin stretched tautly across her skull. Here was her answer. Here it was in stone-cold fact. Pamela had left her father for Drummond Foxley-Daggart! She could not believe it. Those love letters her mother had written, hadn't they meant anything? Oh, heaven, poor Daddy. Tears filled Blythe's eyes, and it was a minute or two before she could bring herself to read any more.

The heartache continued, the pleas for her return that Pamela never saw. *Drummond's wife and son have left him. My Pamela will never come back now.*

And then, *I met Drummond today. He gloated over the fact that he now has my wife. And I know she's not the first to fall for his smooth charm. Nor will she be the last. I don't believe that he wants to marry her, even though she's asked me for a divorce. It was very satisfying knocking him flat.*

More in the same vein, then, *Pamela's ill. I saw her today, she looked awful. I asked her to come home.*

The next week. *A miracle has happened. Pamela's come back to me. But she's just a shadow. I'm worried. She won't see the doctor.*

A day or two later. *Pamela admitted Drummond turned her out when she was no longer of any use to him in his bed. I can't stop crying. Just as soon as I can leave her for a few hours, I'm going to kill him.*

In the days that followed Blythe read that the doctor was called and he immediately sent her to hospital. But it was too late. The mysterious illness killed her.

My beautiful Pamela died today. The page was smudged with tears. *I thank God for these last precious days together. God bless you, Pamela, may you rest now in peace.*

Blythe closed the diary and rested her head on her arms and sobbed. Her father had told her none of this. Just what sort of a man had Drummond Foxley-Daggart been that he could wield this sort of power over women? Pamela's love for Peter had been so definite and so strong, and yet she had gone to this man, willingly it seemed. *As she herself had once fallen prey to Coburn's charms!* And was in danger of doing so again.

The thought sickened her and she sat up, dashing away her tears. She suddenly understood her father's diary entry. *I'm going to have to send Blythe away. I couldn't bear for it to happen all over again. God forgive me, but it's for the best.*

And Betty Rees had said that all the Foxley-Daggart men down the years had been the same. Notorious for their affairs, every single one of them. Never content with one woman. Had Betty known about her mother? It seemed likely. She had clammed up immediately when asked why her father hadn't liked Drummond Foxley-Daggart.

Blythe's heart ached as well as her head when she made her way to her room and threw herself down on the bed. Only one thing was clear in her mind. She would never, ever sell to Coburn Daggart now. He could take a running jump into the nearest lake and she would willingly tie a brick round his neck.

He was as devious and sly as the rest of his family. A little affair on the side while he persuaded her to sell him her land. Oh, yes, he'd had it all planned. She had been so eager and willing to go out with him eleven years ago, showing him by every word and action that she was in love with him, and if it hadn't been for her father's diaries, she might have—— It did not bear thinking about. She felt actually physically sick and went through to the bathroom, where she remained until the feeling of nausea passed.

The phone rang again and still she ignored it. She was in no mood to talk to anyone at the moment.

Blythe ate nothing else that day and she would have eaten nothing on Monday either if Betty had not come to see her. 'Mercy me,' said the woman at once. 'What have you been doing? You look awful. Is your head worse?'

'No,' said Blythe at once. 'I've found out why my father wouldn't sell to Drummond Foxley-Daggart.'

'Oh,' said Betty Rees. 'I'm sorry.'

'Don't be. I wish you'd told me. What bastards those Foxley-Daggarts are.'

'Blythe!' Betty was scandalised by such strong language.

'I'm sorry, Betty, but it really makes my blood boil. And to think I was in danger of losing my head again. Damn! I could——' She tailed off, shaking her fists angrily in the air. 'I could swing for him, I really could.'

'In all fairness,' said the older woman soothingly, 'Coburn himself hasn't done anything, except try to buy you out.'

'You're wrong there, Betty. He took my heart and broke it eleven years ago. I've never forgiven him. He just used me to amuse himself and then dumped me. It's in his blood. He can call himself what the hell he likes, but he's still a Foxley-Daggart, and the whole stinking line of them ought to rot in hell.'

Betty shook her head. 'Sit down, Blythe, love, I'll make you a nice cup of tea, and perhaps you ought to take a couple of those tablets the doctor left. They might calm you down.'

'*Calm me down?*' Blythe almost shrieked. 'I don't want to be calmed down. My mother died because of Coburn's father. He has a lot to answer for.'

'Drummond Foxley-Daggart wasn't to blame for her death.'

'Wasn't he? How do we know she didn't pick up the bug while she was there? The dirty stinking rotten bas——'

'*Blythe!*'

With a grimace Blythe shut up, sinking on to a kitchen chair and feeling suddenly utterly spent.

Betty made the tea and they sat sipping it together. Blythe managed to nibble a biscuit, and when the phone rang Betty went to answer it.

Blythe could hear her in the hall. 'Yes. She's all right. Of course she is. No. No, I don't think so. Yes, I'll tell her. Thank you for calling. Goodbye.'

'Who was that?'

The big woman's brows lifted. 'Daggart.'

'The rat! What did he want?'

'He wondered how you were. Says he phoned yesterday and got no answer.' Betty frowned. 'Were you out?'

'I wasn't speaking to anyone.'

Betty pushed her face up closer to Blythe's. 'How did you find out about your mother?'

Blythe shrugged. 'It was in my father's diaries.'

The woman's eyes widened. 'He wrote it all down? I didn't know.'

'I'm glad he did. You'd never have told me, would you? Nor anyone else. Ben didn't give me a clue. He said he had no idea why my father wouldn't sell. What did you think, that I wouldn't be able to accept it?'

'It's over and done with,' said Betty, trying to sound matter-of-fact. 'There's no point in harping on about the past.'

'But I could have made the same mistake, don't you see that? On the surface, Coburn's a very attractive man. There's no clue to the devious, cunning brain that sits in that skull of his.'

'At least you can see through him,' said Betty. 'Your mother was more impressionable. She loved passionately, and don't ever think that she didn't love your father. She did. What she felt for that Foxley-Daggart man was something different. He had this strange sort of power over women, I can't exactly explain it.'

Blythe could. Coburn possessed it too. 'And the swine finished with her the moment she became ill,' she said vehemently.

'At least your father took her back. She didn't die alone.'

Blythe swallowed hard. 'He loved her so much.'

Betty nodded. 'What are you going to do about this place now? Ben was asking me this morning if you'd said anything. We're real worried about having to find somewhere else to live.'

'Tell Ben,' said Blythe firmly, 'that I'm not selling. I'm going to stay and I'm going to make a go of this business if it kills me. I'll show Coburn Daggart that it isn't always the big boys who get the best results.'

Later that day Blythe phoned Alan Ridsdale and asked him to send Coburn a letter telling him that she had no intention of selling, now or ever, and she did not want him to get in touch with her again.

Two days later Coburn turned up on her doorstep. He looked more fiercely angry than she had ever seen him. 'Didn't you get my solicitor's letter?' Blythe asked sharply.

'That's why I'm here. May I come in?' He did not wait for her answer, pushing past her so that she had no alternative but to close the door and follow him through to her living-room.

He turned then and faced her. 'What's it all about?'

Blythe's eyes were a brilliant hostile blue. 'Wasn't the letter clear? I'm not selling.'

'That much I gathered. What I want to know is why you don't want to see me again?' He spoke through his teeth and his fingers were curled and one booted foot tapped on the floor.

'As far as I'm concerned, Mr Daggart, we only ever had a business relationship. You were waiting for my answer about the land. Now you have it.'

The cold grey eyes bore into her. 'You don't feel anything else for me? Nothing at all?'

Blythe boldly countered his stare. 'Nothing.' He sounded as though he couldn't believe it. How big-headed he was.

'I've half a mind to put that to the test.'

Blythe felt a flutter in her stomach like a butterfly trying to escape.

'But I won't.' His lip curled derisively. 'Don't think you've seen the last of me, though. You should know now that I never give up without a struggle.'

'Are you talking about me or the business?' she asked with a disdainful lift of her fine brows.

A faint smile curved the corners of his mouth. 'Perhaps both, who knows?'

'Maybe my solicitor didn't make it very clear?' She looked at him coldly and wished he hadn't worn those black cords. They brought back memories of an idyllic picnic lunch that she would far rather forget. He seemed to always wear them at highlights in their relationship. Like the lunch, and the accident, and now. Perhaps they spelt danger? Perhaps she ought to beware whenever she saw him in them? And what foolish thoughts she was entertaining.

'It's my intention to get Berry's Cider back on its feet,' she went on. 'I'll work day and night to that end if necessary. And it will leave me no time for personal relationships.'

'You'll kill yourself.'

'I won't. Ben will help me. We'll pull through, you'll see.'

'Ben?' he asked scathingly. 'You need someone young, with fresh ideas and brains and ability to carry them through. Ben's all right, but he's past it.'

'Someone like yourself, you mean?'

'I don't reckon I've done badly in the last eleven years.'

'You've certainly made a name for yourself, I'll grant you that,' she said tersely, 'but so too did your father, and probably his father before him, and so on right back into their dark and lurid past.'

'I don't think we're talking about the same thing,' he said harshly. 'What my father did has nothing to do with me.'

'Hasn't it?' she flashed. 'I think it has an awful lot to do with you. Shall I tell you something, Coburn Daggart, before you leave? Something that sticks in my craw every time I think about it?'

He eyed her almost with uninterest, and she could have spat in his eye.

'That woman your father wanted to marry, whose family life he wrecked——' Her eyes grew colder and colder. 'She was my mother. Now do you understand?'

A shudder racked through him. 'I didn't know,' he said quietly. 'I truly didn't know.'

Blythe could see that he spoke the truth. 'Will you now please go?' Her grim expression and the firm tone in her voice told him that she was serious, that this wasn't the time to protest it had nothing to do with him.

'I'm sorry, Blythe.' He turned and left, and she did not even look at him.

Blythe could not settle once he had gone. She paced the house like a caged animal seeking escape. How she wished her father had told her what had happened. He could have explained as soon as she was old enough to understand.

Perhaps he had been ashamed? Perhaps he had felt that somehow it was his fault Pamela had left him? Perhaps he felt that he had not been a good enough husband? But Kate had been happy enough. There had been no problems in their marriage.

No, it wasn't her father who had been at fault. It was the Foxley-Daggarts who were to blame, and Coburn was as guilty as the rest. In one way she was glad that she had already experienced his callousness. It helped her see exactly what type of man he was. And she never wanted to see him again.

How she got through the rest of the day Blythe did not know. She took one of the sleeping pills the doctor had left, and awoke the next morning feeling ready to do battle with the whole world.

She ate a hearty breakfast of bacon, sausage and egg and then shut herself in her father's office. Very carefully she went through the old order books, checking which customers they had lost, listing them, planning to contact them to find out whose cider they were buying now. She was sure she knew what the answer would be. And somehow she had to talk them into coming back to her.

Their sales area was within a thirty-mile radius. They did not produce enough cider to sell any further afield. Not like Druid's who, she imagined, sold the length and breadth of the country.

She debated whether to send out letters, make phone calls, or pay personal visits. In the end she decided on the latter. It took Blythe most of the day to list the outlets and sort in which order she would visit them, but when she had done it she felt better. In fact, as she grilled a lamb chop for her supper, she was actually singing to herself.

But when she began to call on their old customers the next day her spirits soon took a downward swoop. 'Your father let us down so often.' 'He failed to deliver as promised.' 'Druid's are so much more efficient.' 'The customers prefer Druid's cider now.' 'We never get asked for your cider these days.'

These were a few of the excuses she was given, and by the end of the day Blythe began to realise that she had set herself an impossible task. Her assurances that things would be different in future, that the firm was under new management and promises would be kept, seemed not to matter. They did not want to know.

She returned home feeling utterly dejected. She would go out again tomorrow, see some more outlets, but if it went the same as today then she might as well give up the whole idea.

Ben came to see her after she had eaten, his smile fading when he saw her woebegone expression. 'Betty told me you weren't going to sell after all, that you were aiming to put the business back on its feet.' He looked at her cautiously. 'Is that so? You don't look none too happy. Has something else happened?'

'Oh, Ben,' said Blythe, welcoming him into the kitchen and pulling out a chair, 'I don't think I'm going to be able to do it.'

His straggly grey brows drew together. 'What makes you say that, Blythe? Betty said she had never seen you so determined.'

'I was—I am—oh, dear, it's just not working out how I thought it would. I've spent all day calling on old customers, thinking I could persuade them to buy from us again.'

'And they won't?'

She slowly shook her head. 'And guess whose cider they're stocking now.'

'Druid's?'

'That's right. And they're getting far better service than they ever got from us. They're just not interested any more. I gave them my assurance, I told them it would be different, but no, they don't want to know.'

It was Ben's turn to look sad. 'That's a pity. Our cider's still as good as ever it was. The orchards are flourishing. We're in for a marvellous crop this year. But what good is it sitting in our barrels? Couldn't we find some new outlets?'

Blythe nodded. 'That's what I was thinking, but advertising costs money, which I haven't got. The business has been going down so much over the last few years that it's only just solvent. If we don't do well this year it most definitely will have to be sold. At least, that's what my accountant tells me. In fact, he's all for selling now. I don't understand all the facts and figures myself. I wish I'd had business training, Ben, instead of wasting my time as an artist.'

'You did what you liked best.'

'Painting pictures on china? It's a great help to me now. Oh, Ben, what are we going to do?'

He grimaced and put one of his gnarled old hands over hers. 'Sleep on it. Have another go tomorrow. I have faith in you, Blythe. Dress yourself up to kill, turn on your charm, no one will be able to resist.'

'Thanks, Ben,' she smiled weakly, but she knew it would do no good.

The following day she did, however, succeed in securing a few orders. Not enough to warrant a success, but it was a start, and she did not feel quite so depressed.

By the end of the week her order book was looking reasonably healthy, but certainly she had nowhere near enough orders to use even half of the cider already in their casks. And with this year promising to be a bumper harvest, the situation was still very worrying.

She had half expected Coburn to call again, and was surprised when she heard nothing from him. Ben and another man began bottling cider once more, and their warehouse was soon stacked with crates ready for delivery.

And then, one Sunday morning a couple of weeks later, Coburn came to see her. It annoyed Blythe that her heartbeats quickened when she opened the door and saw him. She had been busy polishing and wore faded jeans and an old T-shirt, and she pushed her untidy hair back off her face as she eyed him, leaving a smudge of dust on her forehead.

In contrast, Coburn was dressed in blue mohair trousers and a silk shirt, and he looked every inch the successful man. Blythe clenched her teeth and glared at him, finally managing to grate, 'Yes? What do you want?'

His narrowed eyes gave nothing away. 'I thought I might have got a better reception.'

'Why should you?' she demanded bluntly.

'I thought you might have had time to come to terms with the situation. I thought you might have realised that I am in no way to blame for what my father did.'

'Of course you're not,' she said with sickly sweetness, 'but your family has a reputation that I find galling, to say the least, and you're following in their exact same footsteps. Don't forget, I've had a taste of it. Goodbye, Mr Daggart,' and she closed the door.

But his foot was in the way, and with a furious hand he pushed it wide open. 'I resent your implications.'

Blythe shrugged. 'It's the way I see things. I can't help it.'

'You're being ridiculous.' He stepped into the hall and closed the door behind him.

He looked big and threatening, and Blythe felt a flutter of apprehension. But she lifted her chin and stared at him.

'Because of the way my father behaved, and possibly my grandfather and his father before him, though I have no proof they were the Lotharios you seem to think them, you're shutting me out of your life. Is that what you're saying?'

She nodded. 'That's right. You're only interested in me because I have something you want.'

'I want your land, yes, but that has nothing to do with——'

'It has everything to do with it,' she interjected icily, folding her arms and staring at him with extreme dislike in her blue eyes. If he had been interested in her, if he had entertained any real feelings for her, he would never have let her go all those years ago. The fact that he was trying again now merely proved her point.

'At least let's talk things over rationally. Hell, Blythe, this is a pathetic state of affairs. You're a damned attractive girl and I want to see you. You're blowing this thing up out of all proportion.'

'I don't think so,' she said distantly. 'And the only reason you're making such a big issue out of it is because you're not getting your own way.'

With an exasperated sigh he took hold of her shoulders and shook her. 'Blythe Berensen, you're the most infuriating female I've ever met.'

She hardened herself to the sensations his touch evoked. 'And you, Coburn Daggart, are the most loathsome man I have ever met.'

In response he pulled her hard against him, his other hand on her chin, forcing her to look at him. There was total anger in his glittering eyes, tension like steel in his jaw, and Blythe felt suddenly afraid.

'Try telling me that again after this.'

His mouth closed on hers in a kiss that was totally different from any other he had given her. This one was savage and brutal, bruising her lips, trying to demand a response.

She stiffened in his arms and stood resolutely still, reminding herself over and over again that he was one of the despicable Foxley-Daggarts. Men not to be trusted. Men who took women for their own needs, not caring whom they hurt in the process.

But when his kiss gentled, when he realised that he was getting nowhere by caveman tactics, when he resorted to tenderness instead, gently grazing her lips with his own, running the tip of his tongue erotically over their softness, pulling down her lower lip and kissing the soft inner moistness, then she felt an unwilling response rise inside her. And, no matter how much she struggled with her conscience, Blythe finally succumbed.

Her mouth opened beneath his, accepting his now deepening kiss, she closed her eyes and pressed herself closer against him. The blood raced in her veins and her heart pumped faster, and she hated herself for being so weak but she could not help it.

Finally he lifted his head away from hers. 'Doesn't that tell you something, Blythe?'

She gave a tiny shrug. 'It tells me that I, and probably a host of other girls besides me, cannot resist you physically. But it doesn't mean a thing.'

His jaw tightened yet again. 'There is no one else.'

'Not at this moment, maybe,' she answered bitterly.

'There hasn't been for a long time. I've been too busy.'

'But now your business is flourishing, you're in the market for an affair. And as I happen to be right on your doorstep, notwithstanding the fact that I own a parcel of land in which you're very interested, you thought you'd take up with me again?'

He shook his head angrily and moved away. 'You're impossible, Blythe.'

'Then why don't you go?'

'Because I have to make you see sense.'

She smiled widely. 'I've already seen it, thank you very much.'

'You're wrong. You're letting my idiotic father bias your judgement.'

'You're two of a kind.'

'For pity's sake, Blythe, I——'

The strident ring of the telephone cut into his words and Blythe hurried to answer it, glad of the reprieve. Perhaps now he would go.

'Blythe, guess who.'

'Bruce!' She put more enthusiasm into her voice than she might have done.

'You sound as though you're actually pleased to hear from me.'

'I am. How are you? How're things? How's the new lodger?'

He laughed. 'One question at a time. I'm fine. Everything's the same as usual. And Sophie—a stunner, but not my type.'

'I'm sorry to hear that. Megan was so sure.'

'Megan's a——' He stopped and laughed. 'I won't tell you what I think of her. I started my holidays yesterday. Can I still come?'

'Of course. Whenever you like.'

'My bags are already in the car.'

She laughed. 'So why have you phoned?'

'To make sure of my welcome.'

'Bruce, you've no idea how much I'm looking forward to seeing you again.' Out of the corner of her eye she saw Coburn frown.

'You said that as though you meant it, Blythe,' replied Bruce in some surprise. 'Perhaps being away from me has had its advantages, after all. I'll be with you in a few hours. Have the kettle on.'

'I will. What's more, I'll have a meal waiting for you. 'Bye for now. My love to Megan and Patty.'

She put down the phone and turned back to Coburn. He was more than frowning. His narrowed eyes were condemning, his mouth a slash of savagery. 'Who the hell was that?'

'Bruce Oman.'

'And what is he to you?'

Blythe frowned at the accusation in his tone. 'I think that's my business.'

'He's coming here?'

'That's right.'

'To stay?'

Blythe had not envisaged actually putting Bruce up, but Coburn's unreasonable attitude incensed her. 'It's my house. I can invite whom I like.'

His raging eyes never left her face. 'Did you live with him in London?'

Blythe allowed herself a faint smile. 'Yes, I did, as a matter of fact.' Not in the way he thought, but why the hell should she tell him what the set-up was?

There was silence for a moment. All Blythe could hear was Coburn's laboured breathing. Then he said flatly, 'I'm disappointed in you, Blythe. I didn't think you'd do something like that.'

'No?' She ran the tip of her tongue over her lips in a gesture that was deliberately provocative. 'Then it proves that you don't know me very well at all. And why should

you? Our relationship didn't last very long, did it? Bruce
and I have been friends for almost five years. There's
nothing we don't know about each other. It will be good
to have someone here I can talk to. Someone who——'

Coburn swung away on his heel with a snort of anger.
'Pardon me, I didn't realise I was treading on someone
else's toes.' He wrenched open the door and slammed it
behind him.

Blythe smiled to herself, but she did not feel as happy
as she should have done. And she wondered why.

CHAPTER FIVE

'HELLO, Bruce.' Blythe smiled as she surveyed the man on her doorstep. He was nowhere near as tall or as charismatic as Coburn, but he was still an inch or two taller than herself, with curly black hair and glasses. 'You've grown a beard!' she accused him in delight.

He fingered it with a grin. 'I hope you like it. I thought it might give me a more macho image? Make me a bit more attractive?' He waggled his eyebrows up and down and looked at her hopefully.

'You'll never change,' she laughed. 'Come on in. Where's your luggage?'

His smile faded. 'In the car. Look, Blythe, you don't have to put me up. That was the last thing on my mind. There's a hotel not far away that looks clean and cheap, I'll——'

'Nonsense,' she cut in firmly. 'Get your case. I've loads of room. It's silly wasting your money.' Having lived in the same house for years, Blythe knew she had nothing to fear from him.

'Aren't you afraid that people might talk?'

'What people?' She glanced across the fields with amusement. 'It might have escaped your notice, Bruce Oman, but we're miles from anywhere. There's no one to see who I'm entertaining.' She deliberately made her voice suggestive.

He laughed. 'If only I could believe you felt that way! But if you insist, who am I to argue?'

He returned to his car and lifted out a battered case and a holdall. 'Lead on, Macduff,' he said cheerfully.

An hour later they were enjoying roast beef and Yorkshire pudding, and Blythe was laughing over a tale about Megan and her matchmaking. She realised with surprise that this was the first time in ages that Coburn had not occupied her thoughts.

But not for long. 'OK,' Bruce said, when they had finished their pudding and retired to a couple of easy chairs. 'So what's really been happening? You can't hide it from me, Blythe, I know you too well. There are shadows beneath your eyes that certainly weren't there when you left London.'

Blythe grimaced. 'My father's business is in a bad way.'

'So—sell it,' he said at once. 'Isn't that what you were going to do?'

She nodded. 'But something happened that made me change my mind. I might have to sell, though, if I can't drum up enough orders.'

'Blythe the businesswoman,' he grinned. 'I can't imagine it.'

'Neither can I, that's the trouble.' She ran a hand round the back of her neck. Her head still ached occasionally. 'I just haven't the experience.'

He sipped his coffee and looked at her thoughtfully. 'Care to tell me what this something is?'

'I don't see how it can help,' she said quietly. And did she really want Bruce to know?

'Two heads are better than one.'

She drained her cup and put it down on the table. 'I suppose so.' And after a few seconds' silence, in which Bruce watched and patiently waited, she said, 'There's this man who wants to buy me out.'

'And I presume you don't want to sell to him? Why?'

'Call it a family feud, if you like,' she shrugged. 'My father wouldn't sell when he was alive, despite some outrageous offers. For a very good reason,' she added pointedly. 'So I don't want to sell to him, either.'

'You could sell to someone else.'

'And they'd promptly resell the land to him at a handsome profit. I know what would happen. I just don't want him to get his hands on it.'

'I see. But by hanging on to it you have the problem of how to make the firm viable?'

Blythe nodded.

'What have you done so far?'

'Gone round most of the old customers who Co—he—has taken off us. He's in the cidermaking industry too.'

'Ah! That makes the picture clearer. All those acres and acres of apple orchards I passed—they're his?'

'Except those in the immediate vicinity.'

'And these customers, they're happy with him, I guess?'

'All but a few. Certainly not enough to sell all the cider I know we can make. We've still most of last year's production left. I can't even see the point in making and storing the stuff if we're not going to sell it. The only fortunate thing about cider is that it doesn't improve or deteriorate with age. Once it's made, that's it.'

'You impress me with your knowledge,' he grinned. 'But you have quite a problem, I can see. What sort of staff have you got here?'

Blythe lifted her brows. 'You're looking at her.'

'What do you mean?'

'My father let things slide, and one by one his work-force left. The few orders that came in, he and Ben despatched themselves. Ben's been with my father for years and is still around. My father did the paperwork. They employed locals at harvest time. And that's about it.'

Bruce's mouth turned down at the corners. 'It sounds to me as though you're really in trouble. The least you need is a manager, someone who knows the ropes, who has contacts, who can——'

'I know that,' interjected Blythe 'But there just isn't the money to employ anyone. There's something else as well. According to Ben, it's going to be a good harvest this year—it's like that with apples, one year good, one not so good, but how am I going to pay anyone to pick the crops and help make the cider? I'm at my wits' end.'

He sighed deeply and looked thoughtful. 'Let's sleep on it, Blythe. You know me, full of good ideas. I might be able to come up with something.'

Blythe did not see how he possibly could, but she didn't want to talk about it any more either. So for the next hour they chatted about old times and eventually went to bed.

Bruce was up before her the next morning, and when she came down he had boiled eggs and prepared fingers of toast. 'I can see you're going to be good to have around,' she grinned. 'I shall be sorry when you go back.'

'Me, too,' he said meaningfully, then at once he smiled. 'Come on, eat up while it's hot. Afterwards I'm going for a long walk in this beautiful country air. Are you coming?'

Blythe lifted her shoulders. 'Why not?'

'I don't know how you could have left something like this behind. Just look at that sunshine. Did you ever see sun like that in Chelsea?'

'Idiot!'

'I mean it. I used to live in Birmingham before London. I've never been to this corner of the world.'

'It is pretty, I admit,' she said. 'Somerset, Devon, Cornwall, they're all beautiful in their own right. But there just isn't the work down here, except tourism.'

He neatly sliced the top off his egg. 'There you are, then, start offering bed and breakfast. That will solve your immediate financial problems. And I'll be your first guest.'

Blythe decided he had a point, but she couldn't quite see herself taking in boarders. 'I don't think so,' she said, 'and you, Bruce Oman, are definitely not paying me. You're my friend.'

'We'll see about that,' he said. 'Eat your egg.'

It was an ideal morning for a walk, a light breeze keeping the temperature down while the sun shone out of a cloudless sky. Blythe enjoyed Bruce's company, and for a while she felt carefree again, as she had in London.

They walked through the orchards and she explained that different types of apples were grown. 'Then they're blended to make the various types of cider.'

'I thought you said you knew nothing about it?' he challenged her.

She shrugged. 'I suppose I've picked up a bit of information here and there. My father was always talking about it. I know one thing, you can't eat the apples, they're horrible. Really bitter, and the juice dries your mouth up.' She shuddered at the memory.

'Like wild crab apples?'

She nodded.

'I know what you mean.'

They were beyond her orchards now and walking along the road that bordered Coburn's land. His vast acres made her fields look insignificant.

'Quite a spread your friend has,' commented Bruce.

Blythe ignored the word friend. 'He's bought it all up over the last eleven years, a field here, a field there, until I'm sitting right in the middle of it.'

'An interesting situation,' grinned Bruce. 'I can see why he wants your land as well.'

She looked at him quickly. 'Don't say you're on his side?'

He smiled warmly. 'I'm with you all the way, Blythe. You obviously have a jolly good reason for not selling, so I admire you for digging in your heels.'

'And have you come up with any brilliant ideas to save the company?'

'I might have.'

He said it so smugly that Blythe halted in her tracks and stared at him. 'Why haven't you told me, then? Oh, Bruce, I could kill you, or kiss you, I don't know which.'

'I'll settle for the latter.'

In response she flung her arms round his neck and planted her mouth fully on his. It lasted no more than a few seconds and it meant nothing more to her than a big thank you because he was going to help, but Bruce himself looked more than a little disturbed. 'You do re-alise that in all the years I've known you it's the first time you've voluntarily kissed me?'

She grinned mischievously. 'If you really can help me, I'll do it again.'

'What an incentive.'

'So come on,' she said, 'give. I can't wait. You really mean you know how I can increase sales?' She couldn't believe it. She had tried so hard herself, and here was Bruce, who knew even less than she did about the in-dustry, calmly claiming that he had the answer.

'Not instantly,' he admitted. 'But in the long term. Certainly by the time you've got your next lot of cider ready.' He spread his hands expansively in the air. 'In fact, you won't have enough.'

Blythe looked at him impatiently. 'Stop joking, Bruce.' And she started to walk again. There was purple and white clover growing in the hedgerows, and wild roses, and campion. He was right. London was nothing like this.

He caught her up. 'I'm not joking, Blythe.'

'You must be. I don't really see how you can help.'

'Such faith,' he mocked. 'Blythe, what do I do for a living?'

'I don't know,' she shrugged. 'You work for a design firm, Longland's, isn't it? But you never talk about it. I don't know what you actually do there.'

'I happen to be their top designer,' he advised her importantly, 'experienced in every aspect of the business. I've been there since I left college, and I've come up with an idea for a marvellous marketing campaign that will double and treble sales, and might even increase your business a hundredfold.'

Blythe glanced at him scathingly. 'Brilliant. You think I haven't thought of that? I just happen to be lacking the necessary capital.'

'Not to worry. I've got it all worked out.'

'Your firm will give me extended credit? On your say-so?' She frowned. 'Don't fool yourself, Bruce.' Her hopes, that had soared so quickly, fell again.

'Not Longland's. Oman Advertising and Design. A brand new company born this minute.'

'Oh, Bruce, be practical.' Blythe shook her head in exasperation.

'I'm serious. I've always wanted to start up on my own. I've got quite a bit of money saved, but it's impossible in London. I could operate from here, though. You can be my first client. No charge.' She made to interrupt but he lifted his hand. 'In exchange for a room I can use as an office and somewhere to sleep. Is it a deal?'

Blythe stopped yet again and looked at him. 'I don't know, Bruce. It sounds crazy, but it also sounds like a damned good idea. You're not just doing it for me, though, are you? You do really want this?'

He nodded. 'Very much.'

'And you'll let me pay you back as soon as I get on my feet?'

'If that's what you want.'

'Oh, Bruce.' She flung herself at him yet again. 'I love you.' She did not see the red car that went slowly by. 'Let's go back now and get things moving,' she went on. 'I feel quite excited.'

When they reached the house, Coburn's Ferrari was standing outside. Coburn himself was nowhere to be seen. Blythe frowned. He was the last person she wanted to see at this precise moment. Why was he here? And where was he now? Snooping around?

She turned the key in the lock and he suddenly appeared from the side of the house. His narrowed gaze rested first on Bruce, then on Blythe. 'Is this your visitor from London?'

Blythe curled her fists and counted to ten. 'This is Bruce, yes. Bruce, Coburn Daggart.' And, with a hard look at her adversary, 'Bruce Oman.'

The two men shook hands, Bruce smiling readily, Coburn merely nodding.

'What do you want?' she asked testily. 'Why have you been prying around?'

Coburn shrugged. 'Just looking while I waited.'

'For what?'

He smiled then, only the smile did not reach his eyes. 'I thought I'd take a look at the competition.'

Blythe knew he did not mean her father's firm. But Bruce, watching them both with interest, had no idea. A sudden light dawned in his eyes. 'You're the guy who owns all those orchards we've just been looking at?'

Inclining his head, Coburn said, 'Druid's Cider, that's me. One of the best in the country.'

'I'm not a cider man myself,' confessed Bruce, 'but I have heard of you. I believe you hold quite an impressive record?'

Coburn looked pleased. 'And I intend to better it. Perhaps you could persuade this stubborn young lady here that it would be in her best interests to sell.'

Bruce glanced down at Blythe and tucked her hand through his arm. 'I can't do that. You see I happen to have a vested interest in her company. There are going to be a few changes around here.'

An angry frown gashed Coburn's forehead. 'What are you talking about?'

Blythe wished Bruce hadn't said anything, not yet, and she tugged at his arm. 'Let's go in.' And to Coburn, 'You'll discover all in good time. Goodbye.'

She virtually closed the door in his face and Bruce frowned. 'Wasn't that a bit rude?'

'He had no business coming here.'

'He doesn't seem a bad guy to me. A lady's man, I would think.'

'Not this lady,' she snorted.

'Which pleases me,' he said. 'And he certainly didn't like the idea of me taking an interest in Berry's Cider.'

'You certainly shook him,' she agreed. 'Do you think it was wise saying anything yet? What if you don't get the results you hope for? We're going to look fools.'

'Blythe, have faith in me. You go and make a cup of coffee while I find a pencil and pad. We'll see what we can do.'

By the end of the day they had explored and rejected dozens of ideas, but Bruce had finally come up with a solution that excited her. It was going to cost money, but he said he could afford to stand it, especially as he had no overheads at the moment.

'You're helping me and I'm helping you,' he explained. 'It's a partnership. Not the sort I would like, Blythe.' He looked at her wistfully, but when she shook her head he carried on, 'But it's something I've wanted to do for a long time. I'm grateful for this chance.'

'And I'm grateful to you,' she said.

He raised his cup, after what must have been their twentieth coffee that day. 'Here's to us.'

'To us,' agreed Blythe.

But when she went to bed Blythe could not help thinking about Coburn. The marketing and advertising strategy Bruce had outlined filled her thoughts to a certain extent, but Coburn was always there and she wished she knew why.

Bruce was right when he said the news that he was helping her had shocked Coburn. Coupled with the fact that she had admitted to living with Bruce, Coburn must think that they were really involved. He would keep away now. The thought, surprisingly, disturbed her.

She realised with something approaching shock that she actually enjoyed sparring with him. She felt alive when Coburn was around, more alive than with any other man. Even Bruce, and Bruce was loads of fun. He was quick-witted and intelligent, and could always make her laugh when she was down. But that physical stimulus was missing and——

Blythe stopped her train of thought. Was this what it was all about? Yet how could she hate and distrust a man and still hunger after his body? What was happening to her?

Blythe did not sleep much that night, and Bruce took one look at her shadowed eyes the next morning and asked what was wrong.

'What do you think?' she tossed lightly. 'I was too excited by your suggestions to sleep. Didn't it keep you awake?'

He shook his head. 'I slept like a log. Always do. And this morning I'm raring to go.'

'Me, too.'

'I want to meet Ben to get a deeper insight into your business, and then it will be nose to the grindstone. This brand new image we're creating is going to take the country by storm.'

'Bruce,' Blythe touched his arm steadyingly, 'we won't produce that much.'

'OK.' He shrugged. 'Whatever area we choose to saturate. Not local, I don't think, because Druid's have the monopoly here. How about the Midlands? No problem about delivery, with the motorway going straight up there. It sounds ideal to me.'

Blythe nodded.

'We'll have Berry's Cider on everyone's tongue. Actually I was wondering whether you oughtn't to change the name? It's——'

She let him ramble on, not altogether listening. He knew what he was doing, and it was easy to see that he would soon be totally engrossed in the project and she would be obsolete.

When the phone rang he was busy scribbling on the back of an envelope and did not even see her leave the kitchen.

She picked it up, and without any preliminaries Coburn said, 'I'm having a dinner party at the weekend. I'd like you to come.'

'Really?' she asked distantly, annoyed to feel her pulse-rate quicken. 'I'm not sure that I want to.'

'Too tied up with the damn boyfriend?' he snarled. 'He can come too.'

Blythe had a pretty good idea what his invitation was all about. Coburn wanted to find out what they were up to. A few drinks and maybe their tongues would loosen. She smiled to herself. Bruce was a teetotaller, and if she told him to keep quiet Coburn would get nothing out of him. Nor herself, she would make sure of that.

'I'll see what Bruce says,' she replied. 'We have a lot to do. I'm not sure that we're going to have time.'

'You'll come,' he said confidently.

Blythe fumed as she put down the phone, and when she returned to the kitchen Bruce looked up, lifting his brows at her flushed face. 'Something wrong?'

'Coburn's invited us to a dinner party on Saturday.'

'Sounds good. I thought he was a decent sort. Never let business interfere with pleasure, Blythe.'

She scowled. 'Try telling that to Coburn Daggart. He's not doing this out of the kindness of his heart. He wants to find out what's going on.'

'Do you really think so?' he frowned.

'I'm sure of it.'

'Well, I for one intend taking him at face value, and I'm all for going to this party. Who knows, maybe I can find out something about his success story. This might be a blessing in disguise.'

Blythe could see there was no way out of it. 'Whatever you do, just don't tell him what you've got in mind,' she said. 'He'll jeopardise it as sure as I'm standing here.'

The moment they arrived at Druid's Cottage Blythe knew it had been a mistake to come. Coburn met them at the door wearing a white dinner-jacket and bow-tie. His smile was warm and welcoming. 'Blythe.' He took her hand and pressed it to his lips. 'You look ravishing as always.'

She wore a mink-coloured silk dress with shoestring straps and a straight skirt. It was a go-anywhere dress and she knew she would not feel out of place, but Bruce? He wasn't even in a lounge suit. He wore a blazer and trousers.

Coburn shook his hand now. 'Welcome. I'm glad you made it.'

Bruce smiled easily, and not by the merest flicker of an eyelash did he give away the fact that he felt improperly dressed.

'He did that deliberately,' Blythe whispered as they followed Coburn into the house. 'He wanted to make you feel uncomfortable.'

Bruce glanced at the other guests in their evening clothes and shrugged. 'I don't get put down easily. I'm not worried, if you're not.'

She smiled at him gratefully. 'Thanks, Bruce.'

He pulled her arm through his and patted her hand, and they moved forward to meet Coburn's friends.

There were four other couples present, none of whom Blythe knew, but they were friendly enough people and there was none of the atmosphere that she had feared. Nor did she know Coburn's companion for the evening. Presumably she had been invited to make up the numbers, because Coburn had said there was no girl in his life, but, whoever she was, she clung proprietorially to Coburn's arm.

He introduced her as Anthea, and she had the most beautiful auburn hair Blythe had ever seen. It was short, falling just below her ears, but it was thick and shiny and Blythe saw more than one of the men present glance admiringly at her.

At the dinner table Blythe found herself seated beside Coburn, Anthea on his other side, and Bruce next to the girl. The other couples were similarly split up, so she could not say that Coburn had done it deliberately. But she did not like the arrangement.

To begin with Coburn was deep in conversation with Anthea and Blythe was entertained by the man on her other side, who declared that he had known her father but never realised he had such a beautiful daughter.

His flattery helped soothe her ruffled nerves, that and the frequent smiles she exchanged with Bruce. But when Anthea claimed Bruce's attention and Blythe's neighbour began talking to the woman on his other side, she had no choice but to turn to her host.

'Is there no way I can persuade you to change your mind about selling?' he asked.

'None at all,' she replied crisply. Wouldn't he ever stop trying?

'I can't see what your friend can do to revive your company. The competition's too great.'

'Don't bank on it,' she spat.

'If he's about to invest money, then he's on to a loser, and you'd be doing him a favour by telling him to put it back in his pocket.'

Blythe's blue eyes flashed. 'I knew that was why you invited us here. All you want to know is what's going on.'

'I have my own interests to consider.'

'Somehow I don't think that our efforts will affect you. You've got too good a name for yourself.'

He smiled. 'Should I thank you for that compliment?'

'It's not a compliment. It's a fact,' she said tersely, and, catching Bruce's eye on her, she gave him a warm smile.

Coburn's eyes narrowed. 'I don't approve of Bruce staying in your house. You'll get yourself a bad name.'

'If people want to think the wrong thing, then let them,' she said. 'I know what I'm doing. And you'd better get used to the idea, because he's going to be there for a very long time.'

He frowned sharply. 'You mean he's moving in permanently?'

She smiled and nodded.

'You're marrying the guy?' he asked incredulously.

'No, I'm not marrying Bruce, but I'll be eternally grateful to him.'

'So much so that you give him a place in your home and your bed.'

'You're jumping to conclusions.'

'And I don't think I'm far wrong. I've seen you looking at him tonight. I saw you kissing him the other day. Those are not the actions of a girl with no feelings.'

He sounded jealous, which was nonsense when all he was after was her land. He was angry, that was more like it, angry because his plans were being thwarted. He had thought he could work on her and win her round in the end, but now there was Bruce as well to tackle, and it no longer looked as though it would be an easy matter.

Once the meal was over and they settled in the living-room for coffee and liqueurs, Coburn cornered Bruce. Blythe watched them talking urgently together and hoped against hope that Bruce was not giving anything away. Coburn could be very persuasive when he chose.

On the verge of joining them, she was detained by the man who had partnered her at the dinner-table, and when she finally got away Bruce was on her own. She sat beside him and smiled. 'What were you and Coburn talking about so seriously?'

'The cidermaking industry, of course.'

'He didn't try to persuade you that Berry's Cider wasn't worth taking an interest in?'

'I didn't give him the opportunity. I was the one asking all the questions. And in actual fact he's invited me to take a look at his set-up.'

Blythe frowned. 'Why would he do that?'

'I imagine he believes that once I've seen how he does things I'll have second thoughts about joining you.'

'But he didn't ask you directly about what you and I are going to do?'

'No, not a word.'

'He's devious,' said Blythe bitterly. 'I don't trust him an inch. When are you going?'

'Monday.'

'So soon?'

'Why not? It will give me a better insight into the industry, and who knows, I may be able to pass on some information to you.'

'If it means investing in new machinery, then don't even think about it. We've got to manage with what we've got.'

'For the time being,' he smiled.

Blythe shook her head. 'I wish I had your confidence.'

'You won't get anywhere without it. Trust me, Blythe, I know exactly what I'm doing.'

It was later suggested that they push back the chairs, turn up the music and dance. Anthea claimed Coburn and Blythe was compelled to sit and watch. It was a slow, seductive tune and they hardly moved, their arms around each other, their bodies pressed close, Coburn frequently whispering in the girl's ear.

'You look as though you'd like to be in her place.'

Bruce's quiet comment made Blythe drag her eyes away and blush furiously. 'The hell I would.'

'As an outsider, I'd definitely say that girl bothers you.'

'I've never seen her before, for heaven's sake.'

'She's quite a stunner.'

'Then why don't you ask her to dance?' she retorted.

Bruce smiled slowly. 'A good idea.' And as the piece of music finished and another began he pushed himself up.

Blythe had not been serious, but it was too late to call him back, and before she knew it Coburn was standing in front of her, an outstretched hand inviting her to join him.

Blythe gave a slight inward groan and stood up.

'You might look a bit more enthusiastic,' he chastised her quietly.

'I don't really want to dance with you.'

His hand on her back pulled her close to him. 'That's a pity, because I very much want to dance with you.'

And, no matter how she fought against it, Blythe could not deny the feelings that sprang to life inside her. She guessed it would always be like this where Coburn was concerned. She might hate him, but physically he was by far the most exciting man she had ever met.

She felt his breath warm on her hair, and to distract her attention she concentrated on matching her steps to his. But it was not necessary; it was as thought they had always danced together, and her thoughts were pulled back again to him.

His finger came up under her chin and lifted her head to face him. 'That's better. I like to look at you, I like to know what you're thinking.'

'And what am I thinking at this moment?' she demanded.

'You're wishing you were dancing with Bruce, but nevertheless you're enjoying the feel of me against you.'

Blythe almost gasped out loud. How did he know? How could he tell? She charged her voice with anger. 'You're a conceited swine.'

'Do you deny it?' he asked, a flicker of a smile curving his lips.

'Actually, the sooner I'm out of your house, the happier I will be.'

His arm around her tightened and the smile changed to grim displeasure. 'Back home with Oman, you mean? I don't like him living with you, Blythe.'

She smiled insincerely. 'And as I told you before, what I do is my business. Why did you invite him to see your plant?'

'Because he expressed an interest. Actually, I was surprised. It's not his trade, is it?'

Blythe shook her head. But if he thought she was going to reveal what Bruce did for a living he was mistaken. She did not want Coburn getting any clue at all as to what they were doing.

'Perhaps you'd like to come as well?'

Her eyes widened.

'I mean it. Not that the presses are working at the moment, of course, but it will give you an idea of how things have progressed since your father's day. It's far less labour-intensive.'

'And all you want to do is make me see how outdated my way of making cider is?' she accused. 'You're still trying to persuade me to sell.'

'Can you blame me?' he asked softly.

Blythe gave a half-shrug. 'I suppose not.' And, then on a harder note, 'But I won't. I suddenly quite like the idea of running my own business.'

Their eyes met. 'Your father lost his credibility, Blythe. You'll never win. You'll simply lose Oman's money as well as your own.'

CHAPTER SIX

BLYTHE saw Coburn's words as a threat, and she freed herself angrily. Her eyes sought Bruce's and she beckoned him to her. 'We're going.'

'So soon?'

'I've had enough.'

'What she means,' cut in Coburn tersely, 'is that she's had enough of me. I appear to have said something to upset her.'

Blythe's eyes flashed scornfully. 'Everything you say upsets me. Just keep out of my life.'

'I don't think you really mean that, Blythe,' he said calmly.

She could have hit him, and would have done if it weren't for the fact that everyone in the room was watching and listening. She had not realised that all conversation had ceased and that she and Coburn were the centre of attention.

'I know that I find you the most infuriating man I've ever met,' she said tersely, heading out of the room, calling goodnight to the others over her shoulder.

At the front door, Coburn held out his hand to Bruce. 'Thanks for coming. I'll see you on Monday at the factory. Come as early as you like.' And to Blythe, 'I'll see you as well?'

And, because she wanted to find out exactly what she was up against, Blythe nodded. It hurt her to accept his invitation, but she assured herself that it was purely in the line of business.

'Good. I'll see you both then. Drive carefully.'

Once in Bruce's car, Blythe heaved a sigh of relief. 'Thank goodness that's over.'

He looked at her with concern. 'I thought it was a pretty good evening, myself. What's wrong?'

'*He's* wrong, Coburn Daggart. He never gives up on a chance to try and persuade me to sell. Won't he ever accept that I won't change my mind?'

Bruce nodded thoughtfully. 'You can't blame a man for trying. I'm glad he offered to show me around, though.'

'I don't trust him,' she muttered.

'Is that why you're joining me, to keep an eye on us? It's all right, Blythe, I won't give anything away.'

'I know,' she said with a weak smile. 'But it's too good an opportunity to miss. Maybe I'll never be able to afford to do things the way Coburn does, but nevertheless, an insight into his methods will certainly be of help.'

On Sunday they went out for the day. Blythe directed Bruce to Lynmouth, where the floods had caused such devastation in 1952. They walked along the coastal footpath to the Valley of the Rocks, the sea glittering hundreds of feet below. Gulls wheeled and squealed, soaring on the gentle currents of air, vivid white against the bottle-green sea.

Goats sunned themselves on fingers of rock, and the only sounds were the gentle lapping of the ocean and bees buzzing as they went about their daily work, or the faint overhead drone of an aeroplane.

The gorse was past its best now, just the occasional yellow flower, whole clumps of bushes dried and brown and withered. There were yellow dandelions and bright green bracken, creamy white yarrow and all sorts of grasses in sweeps of pink and green and red.

And above them the rocks were overpowering, giving the impression that they were ready to tumble. But the overall feeling was one of peace. Blythe contrarily wished it was Coburn who had accompanied her on this walk.

It was annoying that he was never far from her thoughts. No matter how much Bruce entertained her, it was Coburn who filled her mind, and not for the first time she wondered whether she was doing the right thing. Wouldn't it be better to sell and go back to London? Wasn't she causing herself unnecessary worry and upset?

'Where are you?' Bruce tickled her nose with a piece of grass.

'I'm sorry.' She smiled, rubbing her nose and wrinkling it at him delightfully. 'I was thinking about Coburn.'

'He really affects you, doesn't he? In all the years I've known you, Blythe, I've never seen you this way about any other man. That's why I always felt there was a chance for me. But I don't think there is any longer.'

Blythe frowned. 'What do you mean?'

'I mean, I think you're in love with him.'

She gasped. 'How can you say that? I hate him.'

Bruce lifted his shoulders. 'Whatever, it's a very strong emotion he arouses in you.'

'But it's not love,' she claimed firmly. 'That's ridiculous. You don't know what you're talking about.'

But later, as she lay in bed, Blythe began to wonder whether he wasn't right. Did she feel more than just physical attraction? Were her emotions involved as well? They were questions she could not answer, not in all truthfulness. She thought she hated him, but was it hatred for his father that she was getting mixed up with? She was no nearer an answer when she fell asleep, and when she awoke the next morning Blythe felt a sense of excitement because she was going to see Coburn.

They arrived at his factory at ten o'clock and were shown up to his office at once. It was a large, airy room in grey and black and white, with tweed chairs on chrome legs, and chrome ashtrays on stands. Nothing like the traditional splendour of his home.

His secretary brought in a tray of coffee, and Blythe was not surprised to see it was the same auburn-haired girl who had been at the dinner-party. And the thought of him spending so much time with Anthea hurt. Was that an answer to her question?

'Bruce, I've arranged for Ken Browning, my production manager, to show you around,' said Coburn almost at once. 'I'll take Blythe myself later. There's something I want to discuss with her first.'

Bruce shrugged easily. 'That's fine by me.'

But Blythe was not happy with the arrangement. 'Can't we discuss it now? If it's business, I have nothing to hide from Bruce.'

'It's—personal—business,' he said with a meaningful smile.

Blythe glanced helplessly at Bruce, but he shrugged. And she knew why he was not going to help her out. But he was wrong. Most definitely he was wrong. She did not love Coburn. How could she love such an arrogant swine? He was so sure of himself, so confident that he would get his own way all the time. He was hateful.

But within minutes Bruce had gone and she and Coburn were alone. He sat looking at her and she had the feeling that he was exploring deep inside her, seeing into her soul, and she shifted uncomfortably on her seat.

Something was stirring deep within her, and she felt cross with herself for allowing such a situation. 'What do you want me for?' she asked tightly.

He smiled. 'We've had no time alone since your—er—friend arrived on the scene. This is too good an opportunity to miss.'

'What the hell do we want time for?' she demanded, wishing his eyes would let go of hers. Were they blue this morning, or grey? A little of each, she thought, and so intent on her that it was as though he was drawing her to him.

'At one time I thought we were getting along well.'

'And we both know why that blew up in our faces.'

'It was a pity, a great pity.'

'If that's why you kept me behind, then forget it,' she snapped. 'We can have this conversation over and over again for the next two dozen years and it will make no difference.'

His smile widened and he got to his feet. 'It wasn't exactly why I wanted you to myself. You looked ravishing last night, do you know that? I've not been able to get you out of my mind.'

He came nearer and took her hands, and she rose automatically. They stood so close to each other that Blythe could feel the warmth of his body and smell the masculinity of him, and she trembled a little.

She felt as if she were in a trance. She knew he was going to kiss her and she didn't want him to, but there was nothing she could do to stop him. It was a surprise to discover that her whole body ached to be held by him.

His mouth moved gently over hers and her lips parted of their own volition. She swayed towards him and he held her, and she felt as though she were being transported to another land far away.

It was a sensual kiss, not brutal or punishing this time, but intent on making sure she was very aware of his expertise. There was eroticism in the way his mouth grazed hers, in the feel of his tongue and teeth. Tenderness she had not expected, drawing from her a helpless response.

The kiss did not last long enough, and she felt disappointed when he moved away. 'Thank you, Blythe.'

'Is that it?' she asked softly as he walked towards the door. 'Are we going now?'

'You want more?'

'No,' she said at once. 'Of course not. I just can't believe that all you wanted was a kiss.'

'Why can't you believe that?'

She shook her head. 'It's—so impossible.'

'You don't know me, Blythe. I do all sorts of crazy things when the mood takes me. And this morning I very much wanted to kiss you. In fact I wanted to kiss you last night, but it was hardly the right thing to do with a house full of guests.'

Blythe felt bemused as she drifted out of his office and walked by his side across the yard. She could not decide what the real purpose behind the kiss was but, whatever it was, it had lifted her spiritually and emotionally and left her wanting more.

The brick purpose-built factory was nothing like the simple wooden sheds her father used to house his modest equipment, and her eyes were wide with wonder and interest as she looked about her.

First, outside, there were the canals, long, wide metal troughs, where the apples were fed, to be washed along by running water to the huge automatic continuous press waiting in the building.

Blythe had never seen anything like the huge machine confronting her, and she was sorry it was the wrong time of year. She would have liked to see it working. It pulped the fruit and expressed the juice—and made her father's methods of milling the fruit to a pulp and using a hand-press to extract the juice very primitive indeed.

'Impressive, don't you think?' asked Coburn, taking her arm. 'It cost a fortune, but will repay me a thousandfold in the long run. We've still got the hydraulic presses, of course, but they'll be gradually phased out.'

A surge of excitement raced through Blythe at his touch. She wondered if he knew what he was doing to her. She doubted it. He was treating her no differently from any other girl, and it was insanity letting him affect her. She pulled herself firmly together.

Coburn next showed her how the cider was pumped underground through wide pipes to the fermentation vats, huge tanks which held upwards of fifty thousand gallons at a time. How could she possibly hope to compete, when all they ever produced in one year was a bare percentage of his output?

Even in the bottling department everything was automatic: filling, capping, labelling, packing. The plant was working and Blythe found it fascinating, but at the same time she resented Coburn's success. Her father could have done the same had he been motivated in the right direction. Why was Coburn's a success story when her father had let his business slide downhill?

The answer was simple. When Drummond Foxley-Daggart lured her mother away, Peter had lost all interest. Admittedly he had gone on for years, but his heart hadn't been in it. It had been a means of earning a living, but that was all. He hadn't wanted to make a fortune. And when his second wife died he had let go altogether. When all was said and done, though, it was Coburn's family who were the root cause of her father's downfall.

When they had finished the tour, he took her back to his office and they drank more coffee while waiting for Bruce. 'I can't think where he's got to,' said Blythe. 'I hope I'm not holding you up.'

'Not at all. I'm glad of the opportunity to spend more time with you.' He sat back in his swivel armchair and surveyed her thoughtfully. 'What do you think of my set-up?'

'It's very impressive,' she said honestly. 'I hadn't realised you'd grown so big. It was never like this in your father's time.'

'He hadn't the "get up and go" that I've got. His interests lay in other directions.'

And he was saying his didn't. Blythe looked grim all of a sudden.

'You can see now why I'm interested in your land,' he went on. 'You can't possibly hope to compete, and it will do me a lot of good.'

'The answer's still no,' she said firmly.

'Your methods are outdated. It will mean a lot of hard work—and for what? Peanuts? It's not worth it, Blythe.'

'Maybe you see it that way,' she flashed, 'but to me I'll be carrying on my father's business. He would have wanted that.'

He got up from behind his desk and sat instead on a chair next to hers, his hands clasped loosely between his open knees, his body leaning slightly towards her. 'I have a suggestion to make.'

His eyes were definitely blue at this moment, looking into hers, impelling her to meet them. The sensations in her stomach started all over again, but she jutted her chin firmly. 'No suggestion of yours will interest me.' Where was Bruce? Why was he taking so long?

A thought suddenly struck her. Ken Browning, Coburn's production manager. Had he been instructed to question Bruce? Was that the reason for the delay? Coburn had been unable to get anything out of them, so he was using one of his men. The warm feelings disappeared, replaced by a surge of anger.

'What's wrong?' Coburn caught her abrupt change of expression.

Blythe's fingers tapped on the arm of her chair. 'I was wondering about Bruce. He's an awfully long time.'

'Oh, I shouldn't worry too much. Ken's probably telling him his life-story. He's quite a talker.'

'I bet he is,' she said under her breath. 'I'm sure he must have much better things to do.'

Coburn lifted his wide shoulders. 'He won't neglect his work. Don't worry about that. And how can you say you're not interested when you don't know what my suggestion is?'

'If it comes from you, it's got to be devious.' There was a challenge in her eyes as she spoke.

'Thanks for the vote of confidence,' he said tersely. 'Every time I think we're getting somewhere you go up like a puff of smoke.'

Blythe's eyes widened. 'A kiss doesn't mean I'll change my mind about you. Was that the whole idea of inviting me here today?'

'Not at all,' he replied easily. 'I simply thought you'd be interested.'

'I was, and I'm grateful, and I'd be happier still if you'd stop harassing me.'

His eyes narrowed characteristically. 'In what sense?'

'The business sense, of course. It's not for sale and never will be.'

'And what if you can't make a go of it?'

'That will be my bad luck.'

'And your new partner's.'

'Bruce is not my partner.'

'I see,' he said quietly. 'I'm glad to hear he's not going to throw good money away.'

Damn! Blythe wished she hadn't let him goad her. She did not want to tell him anything at all about her arrangements with Bruce.

'So how are you going to profit without a financial injection?'

Blythe lifted her chin. 'That's my business.'

'Interesting,' he said thoughtfully. 'Very interesting. But just in case it all falls through, whatever the idea is, and just in case you feel that my idea might be a better one, why don't you hear me out?'

Blythe could not help smiling. 'You're insistent, if nothing else. Carry on. It will do no harm. But I can tell you now that my answer will be no.'

He shook his head, as if unable to understand her continued resistance. 'If you won't sell me the land— then perhaps you'd sell me your apples?' He paused a moment for his words to sink in. 'You could still live in your house, still tend your orchards, and at the end of the year you'd be guaranteed a handsome profit. I already have several farmers who grow apples for me on a contract basis.'

Blythe was saved answering by Ken and Bruce coming into the room. The two men were smiling and looked as though they had got on well together. 'Sorry it took so long,' apologised Ken.

'I'm afraid I asked a lot of questions,' confessed Bruce self-consciously. 'It was most fascinating. I had no idea your company was so big. The equipment itself must have cost tens of thousands.'

Coburn nodded. 'But it's money well spent. Turnover's increasing every year. Pretty soon no one will be able to match us.' He watched Bruce closely as he spoke.

'You're probably right,' said Bruce sincerely. 'I'm very impressed. Thank you for giving up your time.'

Blythe rose from her chair. 'Yes. Thanks again, Coburn. It was very interesting. Ready, Bruce?'

'You haven't given me your answer,' said Coburn firmly.

'Do you really need one?' she asked with an impertinent smile.

'You're saying no again?' He looked suddenly cross.

'That's right. For ever and ever.'

In the car, Bruce said, 'What was all that about?'

Blythe shrugged. 'Another one of his takeover bids, although in a slightly different vein.'

He looked at her curiously.

'If I won't sell the land, he'd like to buy my apples instead.'

Bruce pursed his lips thoughtfully. 'It would have been a solution if you hadn't decided to revive your father's business.'

She sighed crossly. 'Don't you dare even think about it.'

He grinned. 'I wouldn't. I'm too excited by what we're about to do.'

'We can make a go of it, I know,' she said strongly.

'Even with outdated wooden equipment?'

'Traditional, if you don't mind,' she corrected, 'and I actually think it ought to be a part of our advertising campaign.'

'You're right,' he said. 'The novelty of it should sell the cider. How about if we have a picture of the press on the labels, and perhaps even tiny models on display? We could——'

He was off again, and Blythe let him continue tossing thoughts around. She was back with Coburn, reliving that tender, intensely satisfying kiss, wishing he wasn't the man he was, wishing she could push the past out of her mind and start all over again.

But it was impossible when she remembered how he had once treated her, and how his father had wooed her mother and then rejected her when she was ill. They were of the same mould. He wanted her now because she was unattainable, but if she gave in to him, what then? How long would his interest last? It was a risk she dared not take.

When they got home, she asked Bruce whether Ken had questioned him about his interest in her cider farm. 'No,' he said at once, looking puzzled. 'Should he have done?'

Blythe lifted her shoulders. 'I thought Coburn might have put him up to it. Obviously I was wrong.' And it actually annoyed her that she was wrong. She wanted to think the worst of Coburn.

During the next few days Bruce was busy designing new packaging and labels, and deciding on promotional advertising for their launch, as he liked to call it. He was tremendously excited and worked long hours, and Blythe rarely saw him except when he wanted to consult her.

But at the end of his second week he was compelled to return to London. 'I have to work my notice,' he said. 'I can't walk out on them. But I'll be back in a month, and in the meantime I'll set things in motion. I'll get all the printing done at Longland's. I'll probably get a discount, and that will save us a bit of money. Then we can bottle some of your stock and I'll take it up to the Midlands to see what I can do.'

The house felt empty when he had gone, and Blythe could not settle. Ben and Betty called to see her frequently, and Ben was cautiously pleased about the new image they were trying to create. 'I can't see it making you a lot of money, though,' he said.

'I don't want a lot,' she said. 'Just enough to live on and be happy.' And enough success to show Coburn Daggart that it could be done. That, she decided, was the real name of the game.

Blythe had seen nothing of Coburn since the day they visited his factory, and she was surprised to see him striding up her path one morning. She opened the door and waited to hear why he was calling, annoyed to feel her pulses racing at the mere sight of him. How could she feel like this about a man who was unashamedly using her?

He wore a charcoal-grey suit with a white shirt and maroon spotted tie, and he looked every inch the successful businessman. It was rare she saw him dressed like this and she wondered what the occasion was.

'I hear Bruce has gone back to London?'

Blythe nodded. 'That's right.' And she wondered how he knew. It was surprising how word got round.

'I thought you might be lonely. I've come to take you out to lunch.'

She eyed him with suspicion. 'Why?'

He shrugged. 'I can't lie. I had a business lunch which was cancelled at the last minute.'

'So I'm second-best?' She made no attempt to keep the caustic tone out of her voice.

'You could never be that, Blythe,' he said softly. 'But it seemed an ideal opportunity. I have a table booked at the Castle and you know what excellent food they serve there.'

The offer was tempting, but Blythe knew she had to say no. All he would do was use fresh ways of trying to persuade her to sell. And she could not go on for ever. One day she would give in through sheer weariness. His tenacity would wear her down. 'I'm sorry, but no.'

'Why?'

'I don't think I need to answer that question. We both know what the whole aim of the exercise is.'

His brows slid up. 'You think I wouldn't ask a pretty girl out without an ulterior motive?'

'Not me,' she snapped. 'I have something you want, and you'll use fair means or foul to get it.'

'If I promise, Blythe, not to talk about the cider business, then will you come out with me?'

He had put on his injured-little-boy look, and Blythe felt herself weakening. She looked down at her cotton trousers and T-shirt. 'I'm hardly dressed for a place like that.'

'I can wait.' His eyes were hypnotising her into saying yes and she weakened, as he must have known she would.

'You'd better come in.'

He sat in her living-room and glanced through a magazine while she washed and put on a white silk summer top and a pleated skirt. As she looped her hair into her nape and dabbed her nose with powder, Blythe questioned her sanity, but it was too late to back out now, and finally she pronounced herself ready.

'You look charming,' he said, pushing himself to his feet and taking her arm as they left the house.

When her heart began to thud against her ribcage Blythe knew without a shadow of doubt that she had done the wrong thing. She would need to constantly remind herself of the danger she was putting herself in.

The Castle was well known in the area, and it had in actual fact once been a castle, although it was now a very exclusive restaurant. Blythe had never eaten there before, it was way out of her price-range, and she looked with interest at the tapestry-hung walls and the bare wooden floors, and the solid oak tables and chairs.

The restaurant was a huge room with no windows and a central chandelier. It could have been forbidding, except that it was divided into cosy cubicles lit by candles, where conversations could not be overheard.

They were led to a table in the corner. Blythe sat down and Coburn took the seat opposite, and as she looked at him Blythe wished desperately that she had had the strength of character to refuse. This was madness, insanity, and could not, by any stretch of the imagination, be termed pleasure. She did not trust Coburn to make no mention of the world of business. He never did anything without a motive, and he must surely have one for inviting her here today.

'Are you missing Bruce?'

Blythe shot him a defensive look. 'Very much.'

He frowned. 'I was actually surprised to hear he had gone. I thought you and he had some sort of an alliance?'

'We have,' she answered calmly. 'He's coming back. Didn't that get through the grapevine as well?' With a smile she took the menu from the waiter and laid it on the table in front of her.

Clearly it hadn't. Coburn frowned harshly, a muscle jerked in his jaw. 'I still can't believe you'd live with a man without marrying him.'

Her beautiful blue eyes widened. 'There's such a thing as a platonic friendship.'

He snorted angrily. 'You expect me to believe that?'

She had known he wouldn't. Not many people did. They could not accept that a man and woman could share a house without being intimate. 'You believe what you like,' she said, and to the waiter, 'I'll have the melon and the steak with french fries and salad.'

Coburn ordered steak too and continued to scowl at her. 'How long before he comes back?'

'Just over three weeks.'

'So that's how long I have.'

Blythe frowned. 'To do what?'

'To persuade you that you're making a mistake.'

Her eyes flashed. 'A mistake inviting Bruce into my home? Or a mistake trying to revive my father's business?'

'Both,' he said firmly, and he ran his fingers through his hair, which had fallen with its customary untidiness across his forehead, raking it back, Blythe watching as it fell immediately forward again.

'Aren't you ever going to give up?' she demanded. 'Haven't I made it clear that I'm not going to sell, either my land or my apples or any other damn thing I might possess that you want?'

'I want you,' he said, so softly that Blythe only just caught his words.

'And you think I might come lock, stock and barrel with everything else? What a very imaginative mind you have.'

'That wasn't what I said, Blythe.'

'But no doubt you thought it,' she rasped.

With an effort he controlled his anger. 'What are you going to do for the next three weeks? Hibernate until lover-boy comes back?'

'I have plenty to do,' answered Blythe calmly. 'I still have my father's papers to sort out and I'm teaching myself bookkeeping. I'll need it once things start to pick up.'

He touched her hand across the table. 'I have to admire you, Blythe. You certainly have guts. I don't think you'll get anywhere, but I can see it won't be for lack of trying.'

She ignored the pattering of her heart. 'If that's a compliment, thank you.'

'But you know what they say about all work and no play. I refuse to let you sit and work yourself to death. How about tonight? We could go——'

'No, thanks,' cut in Blythe, and their first course arrived. She was aware of Coburn watching her as she spooned up the melon, but she ate steadily and pretended not to notice.

As soon as she had finished, though, and the waiter had cleared away their dishes, he said again, 'I want to see you, Blythe.'

And in all truthfulness Blythe knew she wanted to see more of him, even though it was insanity. He was good company and, so long as she was on her guard, what harm was there in it? Why sit at home waiting for Bruce, declaring that she had plenty to keep her busy? There was nothing to be done. And the bookkeeping; well, she had bought a book on the subject, but Bruce was competent and he would be able to teach her whatever she needed to know.

Coburn could see her weakening. 'If not tonight, how about tomorrow? The factory's closed on Saturdays; we could go out for the whole day. On my boat, if you like. Are you a good sailor?'

Blythe's eyes widened, becoming deep pools of blue. 'What sort of boat?'

'A beautiful lady. A thirty-five-foot cruiser. She's magnificent.'

He sounded proud of her, and Blythe could not help a quickening of interest. 'Where do you keep it?'

'Salcombe. I know it's quite a way and we'd need to set off early. But I prefer the Channel to the Atlantic. What do you say?'

After a moment's hesitation, a moment struggling with her conscience, Blythe nodded. 'I'll come.' Why was she always so weak where he was concerned?

He took her hand again. 'You won't regret it.'

Blythe was not so sure, but there was no going back. They finished their meal and he took her home, expressing sorrow that he could stay with her no longer. 'But I'll be here at eight in the morning, and don't worry about food. I'll bring everything we need.'

By the time eight o'clock came Blythe was feeling quite excited. Apart from the odd river cruise and channel crossing, she had never been on a boat. Certainly not a private, expensive cabin cruiser.

She wore white jeans and trainers and a lemon-yellow suntop. She had packed her bikini, in case they went swimming, and a baggy sweatshirt in case it was cold out on the water. Her hair was tied back with a white ribbon and her face was free of make-up.

'You look the way you did when I first met you,' he grinned as she opened the door to him.

He looked good himself in navy trousers and white shirt, his hair glinting like gold in the warm morning sun.

'Are you ready?' Blythe nodded. 'Then let's go.' He slung her bag into the back of his Ferrari and climbed in beside her, and Blythe was immediately aware of his magnetism—and the enormity of the mistake she had just made. He would draw her to him as inevitably as a moth to flame. He had that power. And by the end of the day—goodness knew what she might be promising him. It didn't bear thinking about.

CHAPTER SEVEN

THE instant Coburn set the car in motion, Blythe turned to him, saying, 'I hope the same rules as yesterday apply?'

He frowned.

'No talk about business,' she answered firmly. Not that it had got them anywhere, they had still touched on the subject. It was inevitable, she supposed.

'It wasn't in my mind,' he said at once. 'I invited you today because I want your company, because I find you attractive, and for no other reason. And I hope that's why you agreed to come?'

Reluctantly Blythe nodded, but he would never know how attractive she did find him. It would be fatal to reveal the true extent of her feelings. It would give him so much more power, something to work on, a lever to use to bring her round to his way of thinking.

And in all truthfulness she could not understand why her body responded so strongly to him when her mind told her it was foolhardiness. She hated him, his family, and everything about him, and yet here she was, prepared to spend the next ten hours or so in his company. What a mindless idiot she had become.

As soon as they got on the motorway he put his foot down, and Blythe sat back and enjoyed the speed and power of his magnificent car. At Exeter the motorway finished, but there was an excellent dual carriageway, and only the last part of the journey took them through narrower roads and lanes. They reached Salcombe by ten.

Salcombe, the most southerly resort in Devon, renowned for its mild climate, its orange and lemon trees, its palms and glistening white houses. It had a Mediterranean air, and it was busy and bustling, and Blythe loved it. She had been here before, but today she was seeing it through different eyes.

It was a noted yachting centre and there were dozens of boats moored in the harbour, their rigging slapping rhythmically against the masts as they bobbed on the water. Coburn's cruiser looked out of place, bigger and obviously more expensive than anything else, but typical of what she had come to expect of him.

The boat was called, not surprisingly, *Druid Lady*, and as Blythe climbed on board she could not help admiring its clean lines. It looked new, either that or it was excellently maintained. The blue and white paintwork gleamed, and there was not a thing out of place.

'How often do you use it?' she asked.

'Not as often as I'd like. I have a friend who lives here in Salcombe and he looks after it for me.'

'It's certainly a magnificent vessel.' She ran her hand admiringly along the polished wooden handrail. The deck was equally as impressive. Not a scuff mark in sight.

He unlocked the cabin door and Blythe went below, gasping as she saw plush velvet upholstery with matching curtains in a very comfortable living area. It was huge, with a dining-table and chairs as well as lounge furniture and a well-filled bookcase. As she explored further she discovered two bedrooms, each with a shower and toilet, and a magnificent kitchen, as well as the captain's quarters which housed a desk and all sorts of sophisticated-looking equipment.

When she went back up, Coburn already had the engine running. 'Here we go,' he grinned. He had donned a captain's hat which he wore at a jaunty angle, and Blythe felt excitement creep through her.

For a time they explored the beautiful Devonshire coastline, but then they went out to sea, until finally no land was in sight and they were alone. Coburn dropped anchor and they lay on the deck and sunbathed. Blythe had gone below and put on her bikini, and Coburn wore red swimming trunks. It was as though they were the only two people in the universe.

His body was hard and deeply tanned, with only a scattering of light hairs, and she was very conscious of him next to her. They had talked almost non-stop all day about anything and everything except the cider industry.

They had discussed their favourite music, and Blythe discovered he enjoyed classical music whereas she preferred something modern and lively. She liked reading horror stories and whodunnits, and he preferred Tolstoy and Greek mythology.

He had been educated at Oxford and held a degree in modern languages. Blythe had hated every moment of her schooling, though she managed to scrape through in most subjects.

Conversely, at art college she had been outstanding, and she had later earned herself a job with a company manufacturing exclusive fine bone-china products, produced almost entirely as potential heirlooms. They had been disappointed when Blythe announced she was leaving, and said she could go back at any time.

Coburn stretched his arms lazily. 'This is certainly the life.'

She rolled her head on one side to look at him. 'I'm surprised you don't do it more often. You have a good team working for you.'

'I don't believe in being a figurehead. I work as hard as the rest, believe me. Probably harder. How about lunch? I'm starving.'

He sprang to his feet and fetched the picnic hamper, and as neither of them wanted to go inside they spread a tablecloth on the deck and ate a meal fit for a king. There was caviare and prawns and fresh salmon. There was baby sweetcorn, avocado and grapes. There was tongue and ham and various cheeses. There were crisp brown bread rolls and plain biscuits, and lettuce and tomatoes and even wine.

'Smitty's done us proud. I must have put on at least a couple of pounds,' Blythe groaned as she lay down with her hands over her stomach.

'She knew I was entertaining my favourite girl.'

'I don't think I can move.'

'You'll get indigestion if you lie there.' He gave her a playful nudge. 'Come on, a few laps of the deck and you'll be fine.'

At first Blythe felt silly jogging round the deck with him, but then it turned into a game and she began racing him, and finally, thoroughly exhausted but much less bloated, she flung herself laughingly down.

Coburn dropped beside her and put his hand over her heart, nodding wisely as though he were a doctor. 'Remember the song about the yellow polka-dot bikini? Well, lady, you're sure in trouble. It's certainly going boom.'

'Idiot!'

'And do you know what? I wish it was me who had caused it and not the exercise.'

Carry on like that, and it will be you, thought Blythe, but she was still laughing. Her smile faded, though, when his hand moved to cup her breast, and when his mouth swooped on hers the only possible excuse for her quickened heartbeat was his touch.

She knew it was playing with fire to remain here when her nostrils were filled with the smell of him, when she ached for more than he had ever offered her. But something kept her from moving, something stronger than her own will-power. The magic of the day had cast its spell.

He inched closer so that the whole length of his body brushed hers, and she became aware of his every bone and muscle. 'You smell good,' he said, his lips touching her ear, sending fresh waves of desire through her. 'Do you use this perfume to seduce Bruce as well?'

But, before she could answer, his mouth closed over hers again. Blythe wished he had not mentioned Bruce. He would be a barrier between them now. And there was something harder in his kiss, as though thoughts of this other man made him angry.

Blythe, however, felt a leaping of her senses, and her whole body became a mass of sensation, tightening her throat, making her arch herself towards him.

'I want you, Blythe,' he muttered thickly, 'as I know you want me.' He was talking into her throat, feathering kisses over her pulse, which raced like a mad thing. When she opened her mouth to protest he said, 'Don't try to deny it. You think I can't tell? Your body's been responding to mine all day. And it is a beautiful body.'

He pushed himself up and looked at her, a slow, insolent appraisal, and Blythe felt every inch of her tingle and ache. It was true. She did want him. He was right. It was pointless denying it.

He ran his fingers with excruciating slowness along the length of her leg, right from the tip of her toes to her thigh, then across her stomach and her ribcage, teasing, tormenting, making her almost cry out with sheer animal pleasure. Up between her breasts he went, circling her throat, then cupping her chin and kissing her yet again.

Desire ran through her loins like quicksilver. It was a passionate kiss that was a deliberate onslaught of her senses, and she willingly opened her mouth beneath his, moaning at the sensual exploration that had her craving for more. Her heart was beating so hard now that she thought it would burst.

'It isn't like this with Bruce, is it?' he growled, drawing away from her for air. 'Tell me it isn't.'

She rolled her head from side to side. 'No.' It was a painful, anguished whisper. She could not explain in this moment that nothing had ever happened between her and Bruce. This was no time for words. It was a time to touch and feel and sense and respond.

'It had better not be,' he threatened. 'You're beautiful, so utterly, utterly desirable.' His eyes raked over her, and with hands that trembled he unhooked the front fastening on her bikini top, feasting his eyes on the perfect mounds of her breasts.

Blythe could not bear to see him looking at her, and she closed her eyes, but when he circled one rosy peak after the other with a tantalising finger, and when his head came down to take a hardened tip into his mouth, tiny whimpering sounds escaped her and she buried her hands convulsively in his hair and held him closer, wanting to melt into him.

Not a sane thought remained in her head. She was all sensation and need and desire, and there was just Coburn and her, and he was caressing her as no other man had ever done, nor would do again. It was primitive and beautiful, it was mind-shattering, and she knew that she wanted him to make love to her.

She let go of his head and touched his shoulders, feeling the strength of his muscles and the taut smoothness of his skin. He too had a beautiful body.

When he lifted away from her, his mouth moist and soft, his eyes glazed, she made a movement of protest.

'You know where this could end?' he asked gruffly.

Blythe nodded.

'I don't think we should allow that to happen.'

'But——' Her fingers sought him again. 'I want it, too.'

'I know. But I also know how you will feel afterwards. You'll blame me, and I don't want you to have any regrets.'

'I won't, I promise.' She was helpless, completely under his spell.

'It's too soon. Heaven knows I want you, Blythe, but this isn't the right time, even though it might be the right place,' he added with a wry smile. 'Maybe one day we'll come back?' He looked at her long and hard and his eyes were deep blue. Blythe put her hands up and touched his face, and he caught her wrists and pressed kisses into her palms, then said hoarsely, 'Fasten your top, let's get on the move.'

Blythe's actions were slow and reluctant. She marvelled that Coburn had the strength to deny himself. He had pulled on his trousers and his shirt and was at the wheel starting the engine. She feasted her eyes on him. His jaw was set, as though he were angry, and his narrowed eyes were staring straight ahead.

She got up and walked across to him and touched his arm, and he smiled and pulled her to him, and they stood like that as the boat moved slowly through the deep green water.

The rest of the day passed in a dream. His every glance showed her that his desire had in no way diminished.

He spoke softly and sensually. He seduced her with words and glances, and when it was time to go home Blythe did not want the day to end.

They hardly spoke in his car. Blythe felt sad and she was sure Coburn felt the same way. She ought to be feeling happy and exhilarated because she'd had a wonderful time, and yet there was this feeling of being torn asunder. Of wanting and being denied.

'I'm sorry,' he said, when he finally stopped the car outside her house. 'I intended this to be a happy day.'

She shook her head. 'I am happy.'

'I didn't expect to feel this way.'

'Nor me,' she whispered.

'But I don't regret my decision. I still feel it was the right one. 'Bye for now, my love. I'll see you soon.'

Blythe felt close to tears as she let herself into the house. It was a ridiculous, stupid, pathetic state of mind, and yet she could not help herself. She took a shower and went to bed with a book, but she could not concentrate and eventually threw it down, staring at the ceiling instead.

The next day Coburn did not call her. Blythe spent a miserable time on her own. The Reeses always kept themselves to themselves on a Sunday, so she saw no one. She sunned herself in the garden and tried to eat, but she had lost her appetite.

When the phone rang she had gone to bed. She ran to answer it. 'Coburn!' The sound of his voice set everything on fire.

'I've had a hellish day. I wanted to see you but I thought it best if I kept away. But I can't go to bed without speaking to you just once. Blythe, can you please tell me what you're doing to me?'

The same as he was doing to her, though she would never admit it. And she was not sure that she believed him either. He was a brilliant confidence trickster.

'I want you to marry me—oh, lord, I didn't intend to say that, not yet, but it's true. Blythe?'

Blythe shook her head in silent agony. This was going too far.

'Blythe? For pity's sake, Blythe, are you still there?'

'Please don't ask me.'

'But you love me. You showed that yesterday.'

'No, Coburn, no. Not love. Need, desire. I wanted your body, as you wanted mine. Let's not confuse our feelings.'

'Confuse be damned.' He sounded angry all of a sudden. 'Blythe, can I come over? I must see you, I must talk to you.'

'No, not now,' she said in sudden panic. 'You got me out of bed, I'm tired. I—Coburn, I don't want you to come.'

He swore explosively. 'It's Bruce, isn't it? You prefer him to me? No, don't answer that. Come and have dinner with me tomorrow night. We must talk.'

'Very well.' It was a whisper, and she knew she ought to say no before things got out of hand. She would end up agreeing to marry him and then her troubles would start. Foxley-Daggart men never remained faithful for long.

'I'll pick you up at seven and we'll go to the Castle. No, dammit, I want you to myself. We'll eat here.'

Blythe knew that in the frame of mind he was in she dared not argue, but was it wise? Perhaps when he called for her she could suggest a different venue? But she knew she wouldn't.

Blythe spent the whole of Monday on tenterhooks, and when Coburn came to pick her up she gave him a nervous smile.

He frowned. 'Are you ill?'

'I have a headache,' she lied, and it really wasn't very much of a lie because it had been lurking in the background all morning. There was no way she could tell him that she was so worried about getting involved that she had almost phoned and cancelled their date.

'Are you sure that's all?' His frown deepened and she knew he did not believe her.

'I'm positive,' she reaffirmed, and they walked out to his car. Blythe said nothing about eating elsewhere, letting him drive her home, listening to him while he told her about something that had happened at the office.

She knew he didn't really want to talk about work, that it was his way of trying to avoid the intense awareness they both felt, and she tried to listen, putting in the odd question here and there; when they reached Druid's Cottage she was a little more relaxed than she had been when they set out.

He took her into the cosy red room, sat her down and poured her a glass of wine. He moved over to the fireplace, resting one elbow on it as he looked down at her. 'Blythe, I meant what I said last night about wanting to marry you.'

Blythe felt her heart start to race. She had lain awake all night wondering what it would be like married to Coburn. It was an impossibility, she knew, and she would never give in, but that had not stopped her thinking about it.

'I know you said no, but I sprang it on you and you didn't have time to think.'

Was he suggesting that she'd had time now? Did he want her answer this very minute? She was grateful he hadn't mentioned Bruce again. 'Coburn, I——'

He stopped her with a gesture. 'Don't say anything now. Wait until the end of the evening. I want you to be very sure of your answer.' They looked at each other for several long, heart-stopping seconds, then he grinned, as if invisibly shaking himself. 'Guess what we've got for dinner.'

It did the trick, and she laughed and the whole meal was a light-hearted occasion, but as the minutes ticked away Blythe knew that she had to come up with an answer. She wondered if she could put him off. She did not want to spoil their blossoming friendship. She felt happy with him at last, she felt feminine and pretty and wanted and everything a woman should feel. But she did not want to get deeply involved.

After they had finished their meal, he suggested they take a walk in the garden. It was a balmy summer night. The sky was still light in the west, tinged with pink from the departed sun. He caught her hand, and they strolled across velvet-smooth lawns and listened to an owl hooting in the nearby woods.

They were both silent for several minutes, then he caught her hands and turned her to face him. 'Well, Blythe? What is your answer?'

She looked into his eyes and her courage almost deserted her, but she knew what her answer must be. 'Coburn, I can't.'

'Why?' The gentleness that had been in his face began to desert him. 'Is it Bruce?'

'No,' she assured him at once. 'It's because I—I don't know you well enough.'

He scowled. 'Hell, how long does it take?'

She hung her head, but he tilted it back up with a firm finger. 'I'm asking you, Blythe, how long? I know all I need to know about you.'

Like the fact that she owned land he wanted and this was one very clever way of getting his hands on it. But after that, after he had tired of her, what then? She would be out in the cold.

At that moment his housekeeper came hurrying across the lawn towards them. 'Coburn, you're wanted on the phone. It's Mr Browning. He says it's very urgent.'

Coburn frowned and muttered a curse, but Blythe was glad of the respite, and when he hurried back to the house she smiled at the slender woman. 'Does this happen often?'

'Only if it's something that no one else can handle.'

'Do you think he'll have to go to the factory?'

Smitty pursed her lips. 'I couldn't really say.' She began to retrace her steps and then turned and said, 'I hope not. It would be a pity to spoil your evening.'

Blythe felt surprise. The woman had never voluntarily spoken to her before. She had always struck Blythe as resenting visitors. As though in some way she regarded the house as her domain as well as Coburn's, and she did not want anyone else there.

'Coburn likes you a lot, doesn't he?' said the woman, walking slowly back towards Blythe. 'He's spoken of you often. He's been somehow different since you came into his life.'

Blythe wondered whether this woman knew that Coburn had asked her to marry him. She smiled self-consciously. 'We didn't see eye to eye in the beginning, but I must admit that our relationship is improving.' And then on a sudden impulse, 'Did you know my father?'

The woman looked wary.

Blythe went on eagerly, 'I know what happened—between my mother and Coburn's father.'

Smitty shook her head. 'It was a tragic affair. But your mother was young and impressionable, and Mr Foxley-Daggart was a charmer. A real ladies' man. Not many women could resist him.'

'I understand that down the ages all the Foxley-Daggart men have been the same?'

Coburn's housekeeper smiled. 'You're worried about Coburn? You think he might follow in their footsteps? He's after an affair but not much else?'

Blythe decided to be honest. 'He's after my land, that's what I think.'

Smitty looked surprised. 'No, surely not? He was always pestering your father to sell, that much I do know, but I think Coburn's genuinely fond of you, Blythe. I don't think history will repeat itself in that direction. He's not like his great-grandfather, Marcus.'

Blythe frowned. 'Marcus Foxley-Daggart? I haven't heard about him. What did he do?' And her heart sank. The history of this family was nothing but bad news.

'He tricked your great-grandmother into selling him some of the Berensens' land. Your family owned quite a lot in those days, my dear.'

Blythe's eyes widened. 'I didn't know that.' She wondered whether her father had known.

'Oh, yes. She fell in love with Marcus. He was married, but she was a widow. Apparently it was the biggest wonder in the world that she didn't let him have the lot; she was absolutely besotted.'

As her mother had been with Drummond, thought Blythe. And she was in danger herself of going the very same way. Her fingers curled into fists as she listened to what Smitty was saying.

'Your grandfather, her son, was so angry because it meant that his inheritance would be so much smaller that he swore he would never, ever let any of the Foxley-Daggarts touch his land. I thought maybe that was your reason for distrusting Coburn?'

'No,' confessed Blythe. 'I didn't know that story. It's just a feeling I have.'

'An entirely wrong one, I'm sure,' smiled Smitty. 'Coburn's not like the rest.'

But Blythe was unconvinced. The story had, if anything, confirmed her suspicions, and she knew now what she had to do, even though it might break her heart.

Coburn returned and said that he had to rush off. 'I'm sorry, Blythe. This wasn't how I'd planned the evening. Get your bag, I'll give you a lift home.'

He did not speak on the journey. His brow held a worried frown, and he did not answer her question when she asked what was wrong. He dropped her off with no more than a vague smile and a promise to ring her tomorrow.

Blythe thought about the story Smitty had told her, and did not see how Coburn could be any different. It was inherent in the Foxley-Daggarts' blood. They had the good looks and the charm to win any girl they liked, and if it helped them get their hands on whatever they coveted then that was what they did.

She hoped Coburn would not ring her the following day, that whatever was wrong at the factory would keep him occupied.

Bruce phoned at lunch time and said that he could hardly wait to get back, and Ben called in to see her and they talked enthusiastically about getting the business back on its feet, but Coburn did not ring. It was as though her prayers were answered, yet contrarily she wanted to hear his voice.

It was Wednesday evening before he finally phoned her. 'Blythe, I'm sorry, I just haven't had a minute.'

'Don't apologise,' she said. 'You couldn't help it. Is everything all right?'

'Not really. One of the vats developed a leak and we've lost thousands of gallons of cider. It was a major operation cleaning up, and there's work on the vat still to be done.'

'Oh, Coburn, I'm sorry.'

He sighed. 'Not half so sorry as me. I don't know when I'll be able to see you again. I intend supervising this thing till it's finished.'

'You sound tired,' she said gently.

'I am tired, desperately. I've had hardly any sleep.'

'Are you going to bed now?'

'Lord, no, I'm still at the factory.'

'You ought to get some rest, Coburn.'

He gave a brief laugh. 'You sound like a wife,' and with a growl, 'I wish you were. If you were waiting in my bed, I'd make sure I got home.'

'I'm sorry,' she whispered painfully.

'Not half as sorry as me. Blythe, I must go now.'

She nodded into the phone. 'OK. Goodnight.'

'Goodnight, Blythe. Think of me a little.'

'I will,' she promised. She would think of him a lot, but always with that same sense of disappointment. She was beginning to fall in love with him, she knew she was, and it was the worst thing she could possibly do.

It was the weekend before she heard from him again, then he turned up on her doorstep, announcing that all was well and he had come to take her out.

'I'm just cooking a meal,' she said, adding quietly, 'You can share it with me if you like.'

Coburn did not need asking twice. He followed her into the house, sniffing appreciatively as the appetising smell of lamb chops came from the kitchen. 'Do you realise I've never tasted your cooking?'

'You might never want to again after this lot,' she said lightly, tossing a few more peas into the pan bubbling on the stove.

One small chop and a couple of potatoes were not much to offer a man, she thought, so she heated a tin of soup which they ate while waiting for the vegetables to cook.

He stayed for the rest of the day, and Blythe waited in a constant state of trepidation for him to demand an answer to his proposal. But he never mentioned marriage, nor Bruce, and after he had gone she wondered whether he had finally taken no for an answer.

She saw a lot of him during the following two weeks or so. He was a charming, attentive, fun companion and she enjoyed herself as never before. He kissed her often, but with brotherly affection, nothing deep and meaningful, and she learned to relax and be herself.

She saw him in a different light and wondered whether she was doing him an injustice. But she was still afraid to trust him. It was her life she was playing with.

The day before Bruce was due, Coburn took her to the theatre in Exeter, and Blythe had never felt happier in her life. He held her hand as they watched the actors on the stage, and on the way home he stopped the car. 'Your friend's coming tomorrow, is that right?'

Blythe nodded.

'Then I must have your answer. I've given you long enough to make up your mind. It's him or me, Blythe. And if you don't know me now, you never will.'

She swallowed hard. 'What would happen to my cider farm if I married you?' she asked softly.

He shrugged, as if it was of little interest. 'Does it matter? As my wife, you'd never need to work.'

'In other words you'd take my land and use it yourself?'

His mouth tightened. 'Are you trying to tell me, Blythe, that after all this time you still think it's your land I'm interested in?'

'I can't help it,' she replied painfully.

'And what do you think I'd do after I'd got my hands on your land? Get rid of you? Declare the marriage wasn't working and ask for a divorce?'

Blythe gnawed her lip anxiously. 'I have plenty of reasons not to trust you.'

'Plenty of reasons?' he asked sharply. 'Name them.' His narrowed eyes were fixed on her face and she wriggled uncomfortably.

'My mother, for starters.'

'Yes. Go on.' His tone was crisp and cold.

'And I believe your great-grandfather, Marcus Foxley-Daggart, seduced my great-grandmother and persuaded her to sell him some of the Berensens' land, much to the disgust of the rest of our family.'

His brows rose. 'You have done your homework.'

'So as far as I can see, your whole family is devious and callous and use their sex appeal to get what they want.'

'In that case, Blythe, if that's what you really think, then I'll be better off without you.' His voice was soft as velvet, but with the cutting edge of steel. 'Marriage without trust is good for no man. I'll take you home.'

Blythe felt tears springing to her eyes, but she refused to give way to them. It was for the best. It was hard, but there was no other way out of it. She could never be sure whether Coburn was marrying her for the right reasons. He had never actually said that he loved her, and if he did she would not know whether to believe him. They were smooth-tongued tricksters, these Foxley-

Daggart men, and two women in her family had already been taken in.

He pulled up on her drive after an unbearably silent trip home, and he did not cut the engine. He looked at her with eyes that were as soulless as marbles. 'Goodbye, Blythe.'

'Does it have to end like this?' She was alarmed to hear the plaintive sound in her voice.

'What other way is there for it to end?' he demanded icily. 'I'm not a masochist, Blythe. I'm not going to carry on seeing you if nothing will ever come of it.'

He was angry because he was not getting his own way. Blythe clenched her fists and jutted her chin. 'You're right. It is for the best. Goodbye, Coburn,' and she thrust out her hand.

He took it and held it hard, and just for a minute Blythe thought he was going to say something else, then abruptly he released her and she got out of the car. And that was the end. He drove away, and she knew she would not see him again.

CHAPTER EIGHT

BRUCE arrived at lunch time on Saturday. He took one look at Blythe and said sharply, 'What's going on?' She had spent a sleepless, miserable night and there were deep purple shadows beneath her eyes. 'You look awful.'

'Well, thanks,' she said, trying to laugh but not succeeding.

'Coburn?'

Blythe nodded. 'It's over. I ended it last night.'

'I see. Looks like I've come back in the nick of time. You certainly need cheering up. And have I got just the thing to do it. As soon as I've unpacked and had a bite to eat—I'm starving, by the way—I'll show you.'

'Tell me when you weren't hungry,' grumbled Blythe good-naturedly. 'I've a beef casserole in the oven and some fresh bread I fetched this morning. I'll help you with your things.'

Several trips up and down the stairs later they sat exhausted in the kitchen. 'I didn't realise I had so much stuff,' he said ruefully. 'By the way, Megan and Patty send their love. They say they're sorry you won't be going back, but if ever you're in London you're to call in and see them.'

'I will,' said Blythe. 'I miss having someone to talk to.'

He grinned. 'You have me now. I've got broad shoulders if you want to pour out your troubles.' He looked at her expectantly.

She wrinkled her nose. 'Not at the moment. One day, maybe.'

'It doesn't do to bottle things up.' His brown eyes were watchful behind his glasses.

'I won't,' she promised. But she knew she wouldn't tell Bruce. He would scoff at her doubts. He wouldn't understand. This was something she had to work out for herself.

She had sat last night and read her father's diary again, the one where her mother had gone off with Drummond Foxley-Daggart, and it had renewed her anger and she knew she had done the right thing. These men were all of the same mould.

They ate their lunch and cleared the table, and Bruce could wait no longer to show her what he had been doing while he was working his month's notice.

New labels for the bottles with a picture of their old-fashioned press were produced, advertising literature and posters, and the *pièce de résistance*—an actual working model of the wooden press, the huge screw and the wooden arm and the platform where the apple pulp was built up in layers inside cloths folded like envelopes.

Blythe was as excited as Bruce and her eyes shone. 'It's wonderful. How clever you are. But——' Her smile faded for a moment. 'It must have cost an awful lot of money.'

'Money well worth investing. Everyone will ask who your marvellous publicity agent is, and orders for new business will come flooding in.'

He sounded so confident that Blythe could not help believing him. 'I hope so, for your sake.'

'For yours,' he corrected. 'The whole exercise is to sell your cider.'

The next few days they were kept busy turning her father's bedroom into an office. It was a big room at the front of the house and would be ideal. It would simply be a matter of having a separate telephone installed. As she would be using the downstairs study they would not be in each other's way. It was a perfect arrangement.

New office furniture was ordered and arrived, and Blythe did not see very much of Bruce, except at meal times. He was arranging a launch in Birmingham for the new-image cider, and he spent so much time on the phone, Blythe was glad he would be footing the bill.

She saw nothing of Coburn, and even though she spoke to Ben and Betty frequently, neither of them mentioned him. Blythe wished she had something to do to occupy her mind, but Bruce turned down all offers of help. This was his pigeon and he was loving every second of it. He was a true professional, and Blythe could see him having a brilliant career ahead of him.

Finally came the day of the launch. Hotel rooms had been booked for them in the same hotel where the event was taking place, and they travelled to Birmingham a few days beforehand to get everything ready.

The conference-room was decked out with posters bearing the new trademark, and catchy little phrases like 'Berry's for Brummies' and 'Traditional Cider for Traditional People'. Bruce had tried to persuade Blythe to change the firm's name, saying Berry had nothing going for it. But it had originally been derived from Berensen and she would not hear of it.

Dozens and dozens of bottles of cider had been delivered to the hotel and pretty girls hired to serve it. They were going to be dressed in the same long skirts and aprons that had been worn by women at the turn of the century when Berry's Cider was first made.

The working model of the press was set in position, for the moment hidden behind a heavy satin curtain. It was going to be unveiled with suitable ceremony once everyone was assembled.

Buyers had been invited from supermarket chains and off-licences. Publicans too, although Bruce had suggested they concentrate more on home sales. 'People like drinking at home these days. They're your best bet.' The Press were also going to be there.

Blythe felt both excited and uneasy. What if they didn't get the desired results? What if the whole thing was a flop? On the other hand, what would happen if demand outstripped production? Whichever way she looked at it there seemed to be problems, and she would be glad when the whole thing was over.

Bruce, conversely, was perfectly calm. He was in ten places at the same time, organising, advising, watching, waiting. He was a tower of strength, and if nothing came of this venture it certainly wouldn't be for lack of effort on his part.

Then came the time when there was nothing to do except wait for everyone to arrive. Blythe had bought a new navy blue suit and wore it with a white and navy spotted blouse with a tie bow at the neck. High-heeled navy shoes completed the outfit. She pinned her hair up and wore slightly more make-up than normal. She wanted to look every inch the sophisticated businesswoman.

'I'm so nervous,' she said to Bruce, who looked charming himself in a grey, pinstriped three-piece suit.

'You think I don't feel the same?' he mocked. 'It's my money that's sunk into this, don't forget. It's going to be one hell of a success. Don't doubt it for one minute.'

And then their first prospective customer arrived and soon the room was full of people laughing and talking and sampling the various ciders. The time for revealing the cider-press and the demonstration had been fixed for eleven-thirty, and Bruce was in top form as he silenced the crowd.

He had talked Blythe into doing the actual unveiling. 'It's your company, after all.' And he was going to stand in the background doing a voice-over as soft but appropriate music played and the secrets of making Berry's Traditional Cider were revealed.

Blythe ran her eyes over the crowd as she nervously waited for the last whisper to die away. Her mouth and her lips were so dry, she was afraid she might not be able to speak. This was the first time she had ever said anything in public.

And there, right at the back, she saw him. His blond hair tamed, his face unsmiling. He inclined his head in cool acknowledgement, and she wondered how he had found out. There had been no advertisements locally. They had been concentrating solely on the Midlands, so who had told him?

There was no way she could speak now. How could she sing her cider's praise when his was better? When he had the capacity to produce enough for the whole country? He only had to say one word and all the effort that had been put into today's event would be in vain. Perhaps that was why he was here?

Horror struck chill through her heart. He was going to speak out and tell everyone that they would be wasting their time giving her orders. He would tell them that the company was undermanned and outdated, and there was no way they could keep their promises.

She looked frantically around for Bruce. He was watching her and frowning and wondering why she had not gone into the carefully rehearsed speech. With her eyes, she indicated Coburn. Bruce saw him, but there was no panic on his face, merely a smile of quiet confidence. 'Don't worry,' he mouthed. 'It's all right.'

All right? He had no idea how she felt, but everyone was looking at her expectantly so she turned on a brilliant smile and made herself forget the man in the back of the room.

'Ladies and gentlemen. Today you are going to see history repeating itself. We talk about modernisation and computerisation. We talk about technology and advancement and a hundred and one other ways of increasing production. But deep down inside we all regret the passing of traditions.'

There was absolute silence in the room. Every single person present was listening carefully to her words. Her eyes met Coburn's, and she licked her dry lips and made herself continue.

'At Berry's we plan to go on doing things the old-fashioned way. We're not going to beat the big boys.' It was an effort then not to glance at Coburn. 'But we're going to produce a beautiful cider that tastes like cider used to. You've seen the posters, the labels on our bottles. This is real Somerset cider. It will be limited. It will be sold on a first-come, first-served basis. I don't intend to expand, not ever. Quality is my aim, good, old-fashioned quality. And today I intend demonstrating exactly how my press works, how we're making cider at Berry's, and how it's been made for generations.'

The lights were lowered, the music began to play, a single spotlight shone on the apple green silk surrounding the press. Bruce had rigged it up beautifully. The curtain lifted and the audience surged forward to get a better view.

Old Ben, who had come up today for the occasion, began to build up a miniature 'cheese', layer on layer of apple pulp each enveloped in its own cloth. Not the proper cider apples, it was too soon, but they were good enough for this demonstration. Then the arm was turned and the press screwed down, and the juices ran out. Bruce explained exactly what was happening.

It was a revelation for many of the people watching, and there were exclamations and questions and excitement. Blythe began to feel a little more confident. They were aiming to sell the cider on its novel value rather than anything else. It was no better than Coburn's, made with his modern machinery, and it still had the slightly acid taste that the older ciders had, but it was certainly evoking a lot of interest.

People who had tasted it before now began sampling again, and all the literature Bruce had printed disappeared. Coburn came over to her. 'My congratulations. Very professional. I didn't realise your friend was so talented. I might even use him myself.'

What a wonderful break that would be for Bruce. Druid's did an enormous amount of advertising. 'He's done a good job,' she said quietly, ignoring the pounding of her heart.

'I've been listening to the comments. You should get a good return on all this. Sure you've got the cider to cover it?'

'We will have,' she said firmly. 'I didn't expect to see you here.'

'You surely didn't think you could keep this little venture a secret? It's been the talk of the trade for weeks, ever since your invitations went out. It was a good idea changing markets, I'll hand you that. The Midlands will be suckers for this traditional Somerset cider image.'

'Bruce has a brilliant mind,' she said.

'Of course, he's the number one man in your life, isn't he? Are you still sleeping with him?'

Blythe was saved from answering when Bruce himself joined them. 'What do you think?' he asked, his face glowing with pride.

'I think it was wonderful,' she said enthusiastically. 'It was magnificent. I never dreamt it would go off as well as this.'

'I must add my congratulations too,' said Coburn, holding out his hand to the dark man. 'Perhaps you'd like to call in at my office. I might be able to put some business your way.'

Bruce's face lit up. 'Really? That's marvellous. I'm just setting up on my own, as I expect Blythe has mentioned, and I can't tell you what this means to me.'

Coburn glanced at Blythe and back again. 'She's told me nothing. I'm her enemy, don't you know that, the man she distrusts most in the whole wide world?' With those bitter words, he swung on his heel and left.

Bruce frowned. 'I think it's about time you told me exactly what's going on between you two.'

Blythe shook her head and held on to his arm. 'I can't, you'd be on his side. I'm sorry, Bruce.'

'He sounded mighty angry.'

She shrugged.

'You must have given him cause.'

'I turned down his offer of marriage.'

Bruce looked shocked. 'Why? You love the guy, don't you?'

Her eyes were sad as she looked up at him. 'It's not enough.'

'Hell, we can't talk here,' he said, as one of the invited guests came up to them. 'But this is not the end of this conversation.'

When everyone had left, they pulled down the posters and with the help of Ben dismantled the press and loaded everything into the back of Bruce's estate car. It had been their original intention to stay a further night, but now they both decided to go home. Ben had his own car so he went on ahead, and Blythe wondered where Coburn was. He had probably gone as well. She had seen nothing more of him.

She hoped Bruce would not begin his questioning, but as soon as they were on the motorway he said, 'OK, Blythe, let's have it.'

'I can't tell you,' she said quietly.

'Why not?'

'It's kind of private.'

He frowned. 'I thought I was your friend?'

'You are.'

'And what are friends for?'

She closed her eyes. 'Please don't keep on, Bruce.'

His hand felt warm on her arm. 'I care about you, Blythe, you know that, and it hurts me to see you upset. Coburn's a nice guy. What is it that's making you like this?'

'He only seems nice,' she said in a tiny hurt voice. 'It's all a front. He's really very devious.'

'You mean you still think he's after your land and this is his only reason for wanting to marry you?'

Blythe nodded and looked at him sadly. 'What else am I to think?'

'Have you talked to him about it?'

'Yes, and naturally he denies it. But he would, wouldn't he? He wouldn't admit anything. It would spoil the whole game.'

'I can't accept he's that desperate. I think you're misjudging him. You don't have that much land. It wouldn't really make much difference to him.'

'It would give him the monopoly.'

'And you think that's what he wants?'

'His family have always been after our land. They got their hands on some of it once, but they're not getting any more, I'll make sure of that.'

Bruce was silent for a moment. 'You're cutting off your nose to spite your face, you do realise that?'

Blythe shrugged. 'I'll get over him.'

'Oh, Blythe.' He touched her arm again. 'What a foolish girl you are.'

'OK, so I'm foolish.' She shrugged. 'But I know I'm doing the right thing.'

Bruce shook his head impatiently. 'How can you give up your own happiness for the sake of a piece of land?'

'How do you know I'd be happy?' she demanded sharply, wishing he would leave the subject. 'He might change after we're married. The men in his family have a reputation for leaving their wives.'

'So that's the reason you turned him down,' Bruce accused. 'I knew there had to be more to it.'

Blythe cursed herself for letting her tongue run away with her, and glared at him defensively. 'Isn't it a good enough reason?'

They were approaching a service area and Bruce headed the car into it and stopped the engine. 'No, it isn't. It's the stupidest reason I've ever heard. Listen, Blythe, I think a lot of you, you know that, and I want your happiness above everything else. If you love this guy, then for goodness' sake don't ruin your chance of happiness for some insane reasoning that hasn't an atom of sense in it.'

She looked at his angry face and shook her head firmly. 'You have no idea. Coburn's father had an affair with my mother. He took her away from Daddy when I was only little. It broke him up. She died shortly afterwards. I'll always hold Drummond Foxley-Daggart responsible. And his son's no better.'

'You have proof of this?' Bruce was fast losing his patience.

'Of course I have proof. I went out with him when I was sixteen and he dropped me like a ton of hot bricks when he thought I was getting too serious.'

Bruce's thick brows rose. 'You never told me that.'

Blythe shrugged. 'It's something I prefer to forget. When I get married it will be to a man whom I can trust, who will never tire of me and go off with other women, who will always love me, and me alone.'

'For pity's sake, Blythe, you're talking like a mindless idiot. Being faithful has nothing to do with genes and things. If a man truly loves a woman, he'll never stray.'

Blythe clenched her teeth, breathing angrily and deeply, her blue eyes flashing. 'Shut up, Bruce. I don't want to talk any more about Coburn, or my feelings for him, or his for me, or any of his whole damn family. Please take me home.'

With a resigned sigh, he started the engine. 'I think you're making a big mistake, but if that's what you want, it's your life you're ruining.'

Lying in bed that night, Blythe could not help wondering whether Bruce was right. But she refused to dwell on it. She had made up her mind and that was that, and during the next few weeks she had little time to think about him.

Orders and enquiries came flooding in, and she spent hours in the study at the typewriter. She had taught herself to type on Megan's old portable—just for the sheer fun of it—and now she was thankful.

Ben began bottling and sometimes Bruce helped him, although he was working on a design project for Coburn and this took up a lot of his time. When he'd come back from seeing Coburn his face had been flushed with success, but since then neither of them had mentioned the other man. They each led their own separate busy lives, seeing each other only when she needed advice, or at evenings and weekends. Even then Bruce sometimes shut himself away in his upstairs office.

The next big event in Blythe's calendar was the harvest. It was late September now and she grew quite excited as the apples ripened and the time for picking approached. The financial situation had improved since orders started coming in and she could now afford to pay pickers, and she felt an interest in cidermaking that had been absent in the earlier years of her life.

One thing was uppermost in her mind at all times. She was going to show Coburn Daggart what she was made of. She was going to prove to him that she could be just as successful as he. In a minor way, of course. She had no desire to expand and be filthy rich. Success, to her way of thinking, was not counted in terms of money. She just wanted to put the business back on its feet and feel happy that she had done it, that she had stood her ground and not sold out to him.

Then came the day that Coburn visited Bruce. Blythe saw him enter the house and go upstairs to Bruce's office, and her nerves started to agitate.

She shut herself in her study, intending to keep out of the way until he had gone. But a tap came on her door and Bruce entered. Over his shoulder she saw Coburn.

Just seeing his face, unsmiling though it was, set every nerve-end tingling, and it was all she could do to drag her eyes away.

Bruce spoke. 'I've invited Coburn to dinner this evening, if that's all right?'

No, it was not all right. She glared furiously. 'It sounds like a cut and dried arrangement to me. Why are you asking?' And she could not keep the hostility out of her voice.

'We have a lot to discuss and I thought it might be easier over a meal. Of course we could always go out, but I have my papers here if I need to refer to them and——' Bruce's eyes pleaded with her to understand as he tailed off, but Blythe knew exactly what he was doing. He was trying to bring her and Coburn together. Some time during the evening he would find an excuse to leave them alone. Declaring they had things to talk over was nothing more than a ruse.

She shrugged, pretending uninterest. 'Of course you can eat here. I can easily find something to do while you discuss business.'

'There won't be any need for that,' said Coburn, stepping round Bruce and facing her. 'None of it will be private.' He did not look too happy at the prospect of spending time with her either, and she wondered why he had agreed.

Blythe shuffled a few papers on her desk and picked up the phone. 'I'll see you this evening, then.'

Coburn held her eyes for several seconds. It was impossible to read what he was thinking, and it was also impossible to deny the frissons of awareness shooting through her. Whatever other failings he might have, lack of sex appeal was not one of them.

When she said nothing more, he turned away and the two men left her room. Once Coburn had gone from the house, she confronted Bruce angrily. 'It won't help.'

He frowned. 'What are you talking about?'

'Trying to push me and Coburn together.'

'Blythe! Would I do a thing like that?'

'Yes, you would, and don't deny it,' she snapped.

He smiled sheepishly and thrust his hands into his trouser pockets, kicking his foot like a schoolboy who had been caught out. 'Someone's got to do something. You've been going around looking as though it's the end of the world.'

Blythe's head shot up. 'I haven't!'

'Have you looked in a mirror lately?'

She shook her head angrily. 'I've been working hard.'

'You're moping.'

'You're imagining it. I did the right thing, and neither you nor anyone else can make me believe differently. Now, if you'll excuse me, I have a meal to plan.'

She had already decided to roast a chicken, but now she decided to portion it and cook it in red wine with mushrooms and onions.

As she worked, she imagined Coburn sitting at her table. It was going to be sheer hell, and all she could do was hope they would become engrossed in their conversation and ignore her.

But she would find it impossible to ignore Coburn. Bruce was right. She was depressed. She missed Coburn more than she had thought possible. It wasn't so bad during the day when she had her work to keep her busy, but at night, when she lay in bed, he intruded into her thoughts no matter how hard she tried to think of other things.

As she sliced mushrooms, Blythe began to wonder whether she could be making a mistake. Bruce had a point when he said genes had nothing to do with whether a man remained faithful to his wife. Maybe there had been something wrong with their marriages, these Foxley-Daggart men. Maybe it hadn't been their fault. Maybe they had been driven to it because they had made the wrong choice of a partner in the first place. There were all sorts of possibilities, but she had been so blind she had thought of only one.

But why had her mother left her father? There had been nothing wrong with their marriage. Who was at fault on that occasion? Drummond Foxley-Daggart or Pamela Berensen? It was a question to which she was unlikely to find an answer.

She dressed carefully for dinner that night. The evenings were getting cooler, so she put on a thin cashmere sweater in a deep rose-beige with a softly gathered skirt in a toning shade. She brushed her hair until it was as smooth as silk and left it to fall about her shoulders, adding big gold hoop ear-rings and a gold chain with a heavy cameo pendant. Because her cheeks were pale she applied blusher, and a greeny-bronze eyeshadow, thickening her lashes with mascara and finally applying a touch of lipstick.

Blythe felt quite pleased with the effect and conditioned herself to be friendly and polite towards

Coburn, but not too enthusiastic. She intended to watch him and listen to him talking to Bruce, to try and assess him, to decide whether he was a man of his word, whether she could trust him. She wanted to, desperately, but she was still so afraid.

He arrived a few minutes before eight, wearing blue suede trousers and a blue shirt. His hair, as always, was falling across his face, and as she stood in the doorway his eyes met hers. They seemed to be asking her a question, though Blythe did not know what it was. She smiled hesitantly. 'Hello, Coburn,' she said. And invited him inside.

Bruce came downstairs at that moment, and he greeted Coburn with more enthusiasm, shaking the man's hand and grinning widely. 'Come in, come in.' They went through to the living-room. 'What would you like, a Scotch?'

Blythe did not resent Bruce acting as though he owned the place. In fact, she welcomed his taking over as host for the evening. She would be able to sit back, say little and observe all.

Bruce mixed her a martini and they sat sipping their drinks, talking generally, Coburn expressing his concern about an arsonist who had started fires at two neighbouring farms in the last month and had still not been caught. 'Keep your eyes open, Blythe,' he warned, 'and report anything suspicious.'

When they took their seats at the dinner-table, the conversation turned to marketing and advertising, and Blythe was left to clear away the plates from their first course and bring in the chicken.

'This looks delicious,' said Coburn, stopping talking for a minute to sniff appreciatively at the steaming dish.

'Wait until you taste it before you compliment me,' she smiled.

'Believe me,' said Bruce, 'she's an excellent cook.'

'And of course you know better than anyone?' Coburn's words were mild, but Blythe knew what lay behind them.

Bruce was oblivious to any undercurrents. 'Indeed, I would. Five years of Blythe's cooking makes me an expert.'

'Is that why you moved in here, because you missed her cooking?' Coburn asked the question with a smile, but again Blythe sensed the tension inside him. Bruce's answer was important.

A grin creased Bruce's face and he wagged his black eyebrows up and down as he always did when he was half joking, half serious. 'What do you think? She's one hell of a girl. But actually, no. It just seemed the right place and the right time to do what I've always wanted to do. This is a tremendous opportunity for me, Coburn, and I'm real grateful for the business you're putting my way.'

'If you do a good job, if you boost our sales,' said Coburn, 'then we won't be the only company using you. I have a good many contacts and I shall certainly put your name forward.'

'This is wonderful.' Bruce looked from one to the other with a grin like a beatific cat. 'Bruce Oman is going to make it at last.'

'I said *if* you get results,' said Coburn warningly.

'He got results for me,' said Blythe.

Coburn looked at her sharply. 'Business is good?'

'Very,' she said. 'Berry's Cider is back on its feet.'

'You sound confident?'

'I am,' she said firmly. 'The order books are bulging.'

His eyes narrowed. 'I'd make sure it's not a flash in the pan before you crow too much.'

'It's not,' said Blythe firmly. 'Besides, Bruce has a back-up campaign planned. The people of the Midlands are not going to be allowed to forget us.'

Coburn looked thoughtful for a moment, then he directed a question at Bruce and Blythe was left to her own thoughts.

The chicken was delicious, as too were the creamed carrots and broccoli, and her blackberry soufflé was perfect. She served the coffee in the living-room, and while the men were still talking business Blythe slipped away to wash up.

She heard the telephone, but before she could get to it Bruce answered. The call was for him, and while he was talking Coburn joined her in the kitchen. He casually picked up a towel and started to dry.

'Please,' said Blythe, 'you mustn't do that.' She had been vitally aware of him all evening, but now here, alone, just the two of them, her senses began to reel.

He smiled wryly. 'Why not?'

'Because you're a guest.'

He stood so close to her, she could feel the warmth of his skin and smell his masculinity. She held her breath and washed the next plate.

'You've already spent time cooking that splendid meal; it's the least I can do.'

'You don't have to,' she murmured unconvincingly.

'But I want to. I've kept away, Blythe, and you know why, but you haven't been out of my thoughts.'

Nor had he been out of hers, but she would not admit this. 'Are you trying to tell me something?'

'Dammit, Blythe, yes, I am. I can't go on without seeing you.'

The strong tones in his voice made her stop what she was doing and look at him. He was deadly serious, those familiar narrowed eyes fixed powerfully on hers.

'I thought I'd made my feelings quite clear.'

'You did, perfectly, but hell, Blythe, I can't go through with it—with a complete break.'

'What would we gain from seeing one another?' she asked. Except heartache? Why was he doing this to her?

'That's up to you,' he said quietly. 'Friendship, trust, affection.'

Was he giving her another chance? Had he at last accepted that she and Bruce were not lovers? Did he still want to marry her, and was this his way of steering towards that goal? Or was it still her land he was after? What should she do? Give in to the dictates of her heart? Or obey her instincts? He had dropped her once before, she must never lose sight of that. How did she know he wouldn't do it again? It was a family trait, after all. She swallowed hard. 'I'm not sure, Coburn.'

He threw down the towel and caught her shoulders hard. 'What do you mean, you're not sure? What is there to be sure about? Hell, I'm not asking you to go to bed with me.'

Blythe looked at him nervously. 'I'm not sure I can handle such a relationship.'

'Why?' There was a sudden stillness about him.

Because she felt more for him than friendship. Because she loved him. And it would be impossible to hide her emotions. 'Because——' Her eyes implored him not to press for an answer.

His fingertips bruised as his grip tightened. 'Dammit, it's not still Bruce?'

'No,' she whispered.

'Then could it be that—that your feelings for me run deeper than you're prepared to admit?'

A scared look came into her eyes.

'Is that it, Blythe?'

Almost imperceptibly, she nodded.

'You actually love me?'

Faintly, 'Yes.'

'But you can't or won't trust me?'

Blythe shook her head. 'You let me down once. You really hurt me, although you never knew it. That's not the only reason, but it's part of it and——'

'Blythe,' he frowned, 'I honestly didn't know you felt so strongly about me in those days.'

'It was just a game to you, wasn't it?' she asked in a crushed little voice.

'Not a game, Blythe; believe me, I was deadly serious about you—until I found out how old you were.'

Her eyes widened. She hadn't known he had discovered her real age. 'I wanted you to think I was grown-up,' she said defensively. 'I hated being sixteen—it's an in-between age. No one takes you seriously.'

'You were still a child and I was a man. I couldn't take advantage of you. Believe me, it was one of the hardest decisions I ever had to make. And by the time I realised that I owed you some sort of explanation, you'd gone to London. It was too late.'

'You thought what I felt was nothing more than a schoolgirl crush?'

'Something like that,' he admitted. 'Oh, Blythe, Blythe.' He crushed her to him. 'You will trust me in time, I promise you that. Give yourself a chance. Give us both one. A step at a time, that's all I'm asking you to take. Is it a deal?'

Their eyes were locked as she nodded, and she mentally crossed her fingers that she was not making a mistake, one there might be no backing out of. Coburn was a determined man, ruthless even, both in his business life and his private life. Please, God, she prayed silently, let it be me and not what I possess that he's after.

CHAPTER NINE

THERE followed a few deliriously happy days, days spent almost entirely alone with Coburn. He wined her and dined her, he took her out on his boat, and by helicopter to the Scilly Isles, which Blythe adored. They went to London for a show and stayed the night. They went to Stratford-on-Avon and saw *A Midsummer Night's Dream*. And in all this time he never once kissed her. Not even the brotherly kisses he had given her the last time they had tried to develop their relationship.

He was the friend he had promised, and nothing more. Blythe began to seriously wonder whether she had misjudged him, and even more worrying were her feelings for him.

They were deepening by the day, by the hour, by the minute, and she longed to feel his arms around her, his mouth on hers, his whispered words of love. But there was nothing. And it was her own fault. She had brought it all on herself. And, much as she loved him, she could not bring herself to make the first move. Once she took that step there would be no going back. It would be a forever decision.

One evening when they were out walking on Exmoor, watching a blood-red sun sink slowly below the horizon—Blythe thought it was the most spectacular sunset she had ever seen—Coburn caught his foot in a rabbit hole and lurched to the floor with an agonised cry.

Immediately Blythe dropped to her knees beside him. 'Coburn! Oh, no, are you hurt badly?' He was not moving. He was lying face-forward and he was deathly still.

'Coburn, please! Coburn, speak to me.'

Still nothing.

Blythe did not know what to do. He was too heavy for her to move and they were miles from the nearest house. There wasn't a soul in sight. She touched his face, feeling the pulse at his temple, but not really knowing what she was searching for. 'Oh, Coburn, please wake up, please speak to me. Oh, what am I going to do?' She pressed her lips to his temple where her fingers had been a second earlier. 'I love you. *I love you.* Please wake up.'

The next second she was caught in an embrace that took the breath out of her, crushed to a hard, exciting body, her mouth imprisoned by cool, demanding lips.

Realising she had been tricked, Blythe beat her hands furiously on his back, but as his kiss deepened so her struggles became less fierce, and in a short while she was returning kiss for kiss, straining against him, giving herself up to the pleasure she had denied herself for so long.

By the time he was ready to let her go, her breathing was erratic and her heart pounded fit to burst. Her lips felt hot and bruised, and she looked into his eyes and saw her own pained desire reflected there.

She was crazy distrusting this man, she told herself. She loved him and needed him, and she wanted to spend the rest of her life with him. Damn the cider farm, he could have it. Damn the Foxley-Daggarts, it was ridiculous tarring Coburn with the same brush. She loved him, and that was all that mattered.

But she could not quite bring herself to say the magic words, even though she knew it was up to her. This was a beginning, though. Their relationship would improve by leaps and bounds. And one day, when the time was right, she would ask him to marry her.

'Forgive me?' A lazy smile curved his thin lips.

Blythe nodded. 'Though I must be crazy. That was some trick you played.'

'I did fall.'

'But you didn't hurt yourself?'

'I don't think so.'

'I ought to hate you.'

He pulled her head down to his and kissed her. 'But you can't.'

'I'm a fool.'

He touched her lips with his tongue. 'A beautiful fool.'

Tiny whimpers of sheer animal pleasure escaped Blythe's throat.

'I couldn't wait forever.'

She pulled a face. 'It crucified me denying myself you.'

'Me, too.'

This time it was Blythe who kissed Coburn, and she poured into it every ounce of feeling.

'Promise you won't put me through all this again?' he asked when they finally drew apart.

'I promise.'

He closed his eyes and a sigh of sheer relief left his body, and how long they lay there locked in each other's arms Blythe did not know. It felt like forever.

When they finally stood up her legs behaved as though they were stuffed with cotton wool, and Coburn was not much better. They clung to each other, weaving their way drunkenly back to his car. Once seated, he kissed her again, and then they made their way slowly home.

Blythe asked him to come in, but he refused. 'I want a reasonably early night. We're starting harvesting tomorrow, and I always like to see the first apples picked. You can come and watch if you like.'

Just a faint sneaking suspicion crept into Blythe's mind. He was trying to impress her. There would be no hand-picking here, it would be all mechanical. He wanted her to see what could be done. He wanted to prove to her that she could never be as good as he. But she squashed the thought immediately as unworthy. She must learn not to mistrust everything he said. 'I'd love to.'

And there was no denying she was impressed. In his orchards where the standard trees grew some six to nine metres tall, the tree-shaker was busy. Men drove special tractors and huge mechanical arms grabbed each tree-trunk and shook it. The apples came tumbling down, where they were sucked up by a huge vacuum.

'Think of the time saved,' said Coburn, his arm lightly about Blythe's shoulders.

Time, yes, but the cost of such a machine made it prohibitive. 'It's traditional methods that are going to sell my cider,' she said primly, though with a smile. 'Bruce has made sure of that. I don't know what I'd do without him.'

'It's a good gimmick,' he agreed, a slight tightening to his lips at the enthusiasm in her voice when she mentioned Bruce. 'But surely the cider will cost more? And price is a determining factor these days. I'm not so sure that you're wise to place all your faith in him.'

'Price doesn't necessarily count,' she replied. 'People are getting quality-conscious.'

'Are you saying I'm not selling quality stuff?'

Blythe's grin was impish. 'I wouldn't know. I've never tasted any.'

His brows shot up. 'Shame on you. We must certainly remedy that. Once we're through, we'll go back to the works and you can sample as many brands as you like.'

Blythe felt deliriously happy. There was a new rapport between them, and they could each say what they liked without the other taking offence. She stood on tiptoe and kissed his cheek, and his arm about her tightened.

They moved to the bush orchards where the smaller trees were grown closer together and the harvesting was much easier. They watched as the apples were gathered up at the front of the tractor, the stones and leaves and other rubbish separated, and then the fruit was elevated up a tractor-feed and deposited into a trailer at the rear.

'We get a yield of ten tons to the acre here, as against two or three with the standards,' explained Coburn.

'So why aren't you growing all small trees?' And would he replace her trees if he ever got his hands on the land?

'It takes anything from ten to fifteen years for a standard tree to mature. That would be a waste.' He smiled indulgently. 'You really don't know very much about the industry, do you?'

Blythe shrugged. 'I'm learning.'

'I only hope it's not all in vain.'

'I don't see why it should be.' Her eyes flashed as she looked at him.

'You and Bruce are like the blind leading the blind.'

Her head jerked. Again that hint of animosity towards the other man. 'I have Ben as well,' she countered firmly.

'He's past his prime.'

'He's still able to advise. And with the money I've made on recent orders I can easily afford pickers. I'll probably even be employing someone full-time.'

'Things are that good, eh?'

'Pretty good,' she confirmed. 'And looking better all the time.'

'In which case I'd better watch out,' he said. 'Come on, let's go and find a few samples. You can tell me whether it's as good as yours.'

Blythe thought he looked displeased about her success, or was it in her mind? A faint frown furrowed his brow as they got into the car.

But there was no sign of it as he introduced her to his various blends of cider. They laughed and joked, and he promised to pick her up that evening and take her out to dinner. Even Anthea coming in and making up to her boss did not bother her.

She felt that she was learning to trust him at last, and that evening Bruce remarked on her appearance. 'You're looking more beautiful by the day, Blythe. Can I expect to hear wedding bells soon?'

Laughingly she shook her head. 'I don't think so.' She hadn't the courage to ask Coburn. Not yet, anyway. But it didn't matter. She was happy as things were. They were steadily developing a solid relationship, and whether it took months or years was of no consequence. She would know at the end of the day exactly what her feelings for Coburn were.

Trust took a lot of building up, especially after her earlier experience with him—and her mother's—and her great-grandmother's! The Foxley-Daggart men had a lot to answer for.

The days sped by and her happiness increased. The apples on her trees ripened and fell and were collected. It was a time-consuming task. She did not have as many workers as she would have liked, but the men and women who did it were industrious. They had worked for her father and were glad the company was back on its feet.

Blythe unfortunately saw less of Coburn, because she was out there helping her pickers, falling into bed each night totally exhausted. But it was the least she could do.

He did not like it and he phoned her frequently. 'Why are you doing it? You don't have to.'

She grimaced. 'This is a one-man business, don't forget.'

'Are you sure that's not an excuse?'

Blythe frowned into the phone. 'What do you mean?'

'I'm talking about the fact that you're there alone with Bruce every night. Is it he who's keeping you away from me?'

The note of suspicion in his voice hurt her. 'Oh, Coburn,' she said, 'I thought you'd accepted that he means nothing to me. He never has. He's a good friend, that's all.'

'Why do I suddenly have difficulty in believing you?'

'I don't know, Coburn. All I know is that you're making an issue out of nothing.' An edge of irritation crept into her voice. This was ridiculous. There was no foundation for these accusations.

'Then why do you keep refusing to see me?'

'You know why. I'm so tired after apple-picking all day.'

'Will you have dinner with me here tomorrow night?'

Blythe knew she dared not refuse, even though another full day lay ahead. She paused fractionally before saying, 'Yes, I'll come.'

'Good.' His tone was curt. 'I'll pick you up at a quarter to eight.'

It dismayed Blythe to find their new-found relationship suddenly in danger, just when she had thought everything was going so well. Did Coburn really think that Bruce was the reason she was not seeing so much of him?

She dressed carefully for her dinner-date in a silky silver-grey dress cut low at both the back and the front. She had bought it in London and Megan always said it would knock any man for six.

Coburn's eyes flickered over her when he picked her up but he made no comment, and Blythe walked sedately out to his car with him. The easy rapport they had developed was missing.

Smitty, as usual, did them proud with fillets of venison for their main course served in a beautiful pepper sauce to which had been added cashew nuts and raisins. It was a delicious combination.

To cover her unease Blythe chatted almost non-stop, telling him about the way her business was improving, almost adding that it was all thanks to Bruce, remembering in time that Bruce was the cause of this tension between them. As soon as they finished eating they retired to his sitting-room. Blythe sat next to him on the settee. 'Coburn,' she said, deciding it was time to clear the air, 'about Bruce. You really have no need to be jealous. There's nothing between us. There never has been. There never will be.'

'I've seen you with him in the fields.'

Blythe frowned. Had Coburn been spying on them?

'You looked happier with him than you ever have with me.'

'That's not true,' she said quickly. 'He's a good friend. A very good friend. And I hope he always remains so.'

'I saw you kissing him.'

'Kissing him?' Blythe frowned and cast her mind back. Then she remembered and laughed. 'Oh, Coburn, it was his birthday and I'd forgotten, so I gave him a kiss instead of a present. All the other women pickers kissed him as well, or didn't you see that?'

'No,' he said abruptly. 'I'd left.'

'But you're not convinced?' Blythe began to grow angry. He was being pathetically paranoid about the whole thing.

'I don't like him living with you.'

'You've told me that a thousand times,' she snapped. 'Is this a reversal of attitudes? Don't *you* trust *me*?'

'Hell, Blythe, I want to,' he groaned, 'but I can't help myself. You're always talking about him. You're always singing his praises. What would you think if I had another woman living with me and almost every time I opened my mouth I mentioned her?'

Blythe could not deny that she would be jealous, too.

'I want you to ask him to move out.'

'No,' she said at once.

'Then you move in here with me.'

She shook her head. 'I won't do that, either.' She was not going to be dictated to by Coburn or any man.

He clenched his fists and pushed himself up. Blythe followed suit. 'Coburn, please, you're being silly.'

'Am I?' he demanded, turning to her. 'Am I? I can't help what I feel in here.' He banged his fist on his heart. 'I've never quite believed your story that you and Bruce aren't lovers, and when you constantly refused to see me I knew there had to be something in it.'

Blythe knew that if she said any more at this moment the whole affair would blow up out of all proportion, if it hadn't already. 'I think it's time I went home,' she said distantly.

It was difficult to believe that she had been on the verge of agreeing to marry him. His insane jealousy had ruined the harmony they had taken such pains to create.

Coburn had always been jealous of Bruce, right from the very beginning, but surely he could see that it was unfounded? And if he couldn't, what foundation was that for a happy marriage? Perhaps it was as well his feelings had erupted before she had committed herself to him.

'If that's what you want?' His grey eyes were those of a stranger.

Blythe lifted her chin. 'Yes, I do. I should never have come here tonight.'

'No, you should have stayed in Bruce's bed.'

Her hand flew through the air and struck his cheek. 'How dare you?'

Without hesitation he hit her back.

Blythe clapped her hand to her cheek, unable to believe he had actually struck her. Then she turned haughtily towards the door. 'Please ask your chauffeur to drive me home.'

It was not until she was in bed that Blythe allowed the tears to flow, then they soaked her pillow and remained unchecked. In an odd sort of way she could see now why Coburn had found her distrust so hard to understand. People believed what they wanted to believe, no matter what facts were thrust before them. She had refused to trust him and now he was refusing to trust her. It looked like the end of the road. And how empty the future would be.

Unable to sleep, Blythe got up and heated some milk, taking it back upstairs and standing at the window as she drank it. It was a clear starry night, the moon bathing everything with silver. A sudden movement caught her eye and she saw Coburn in the yard. What the hell was he doing here? Surely he hadn't come to continue their argument?'

Bruce was out on a date with a girl he had met recently, or she would have called him to send Coburn away. Angrily she pulled on her dressing-gown and ran downstairs, but when she opened the door he was not there. She called and searched and there wasn't a soul about, only the sound of a car engine fading into the distance.

A deep frown creased Blythe's brow as she returned to her bedroom, standing at the window for a moment before climbing back into bed. What game was he playing? Or had it been imagination? A trick of the light? A shadow? He was so much on her mind that she was seeing him when he wasn't there.

In minutes she was asleep and she had no idea how long it was before she woke and her room was bathed in a golden glow. Morning already? she groaned, before realising that the light was not from the sun.

The flickering colour was accompanied by fierce crackling, and her nostrils were abused by the smell of woodsmoke. Alarm tightened her throat and she jumped out of bed. Her first thoughts were that the house was on fire, but through her window she saw that it was the wooden building that housed the press.

Blythe raced from her room and pushed open Bruce's door, but he wasn't home yet. She went into his office and snatched up the phone to alert the fire brigade. But it would be ages before they got here. She must do something.

Outside she fixed the garden hose on a tap and played it over the flaming building, but it was all in vain. It was already well alight. All she could do was stand and watch as her hopes and dreams for the future were burned to the ground.

When Ben joined her, tears were streaming down her face. 'What's happened?' he asked harshly. 'How did it start?'

'I was asleep,' she choked, though in her mind she knew exactly who had started it.

At that moment the fire engine screamed into sight and soon the flames were doused and all that remained was acrid, sickly smoke. The precious press had gone, reduced to a pile of charred timber, criss-crossed with fallen beams from the building.

Blythe could not take her eyes off it, and hatred as white-hot as the heart of the fire ripped through her. It was difficult to believe Coburn would go to such lengths, but what else could she think? She had seen him with her own eyes. And all because he thought she was sleeping with Bruce!

Was he really so hurt by it that he would ruin her chances of success? Or was it in fact her success that bothered him? Or even, perhaps, a combination of both? She and Bruce were building up a firm he had thought doomed. They were a team. And, since she refused to split up from Bruce, this was his way of making sure that she did. And, of course, she would have no choice but to sell up. There was no way she could start all over again.

She swung about and went into the house, got dressed and picked up her car keys. Half-way to Coburn's house, she changed her mind and headed for the police station instead. Fighting verbally with Coburn would get her nowhere. She wanted justice, and she didn't want him forewarned.

But it was not so easy. 'No, I can't be sure it was him who started the fire,' she said yet again. 'I saw him in the yard earlier. No, I didn't actually see his face. But it was Coburn, I know it was.'

She was there for over an hour, and they promised to go and see Coburn, but they made her realise that without proof there was not very much they could do. Coburn was such a well-known and well-respected figure in the area that it was doubtful her complaint would stick.

Blythe waited for the police to call her. She sat in the kitchen and drank cup after cup of coffee. How dared they say it wasn't Coburn when she had seen him with her own eyes?

Bruce returned at about two in the morning, and he was white-faced when he let himself into the house. 'Blythe, I can't believe what I've just seen. I take it the arsonist's been at it again?'

'Arsonist be damned,' she flashed. 'Coburn set it on fire.'

'Coburn?' he echoed incredulously.

She nodded. 'That's right.'

'He wouldn't do a thing like that.'

'Wouldn't he?' she demanded strongly. 'You'd jolly well better believe it, because I saw him, and I've been to the police. They're going to charge him.'

'Blythe!' gasped Bruce. 'Are you sure?'

'Of course I'm sure. I'm waiting for their call now to say they're going to arrest him. And it's no more than he deserves.'

Bruce shook his head and lowered himself on to a chair, pouring a cup of coffee from the pot on the table. 'You'd better tell me exactly what happened.'

'I've already told the police,' she said tersely. 'I don't feel like going through it all again.'

He took a gulp of the steaming liquid. 'You actually saw Coburn setting fire to the building?'

She lifted her shoulders. 'Not exactly. But he was out there earlier.'

'You spoke to him?'

'No, I saw him from my bedroom window.'

'And you recognised Coburn in the dark?'

She flashed her blue eyes. 'You sound like the police.'

'And I'm sure they're equally as sceptical. Blythe, he could sue you for slander if you're wrong. You do realise that?'

She sank her head into her hands. 'I've lost everything. I worked so hard. *You* worked so hard. We were just ready to press the apples, and now—nothing. *Nothing*. Oh, Bruce, what am I going to do?'

He stood up and put his hands on her shoulders. 'What you're going to do, Blythe, right at this moment, is go to bed.'

'I couldn't,' she cried. 'I wouldn't sleep. All I can see every time I close my eyes are flames leaping into the air. I can still smell it, can't you? I shall have nightmares about tonight for the rest of my life.'

'No, you won't,' he said gently. 'It won't seem half so bad in the morning. Come on, let me take you up.'

At that moment the telephone shrilled. 'Yes? I'm not surprised. Thank you. I'll be here. Goodbye.'

'The police?' asked Bruce gently.

She nodded. 'Coburn obviously said it wasn't him. He has the perfect excuse, hasn't he, with that arsonist in the area? But they're going to interview him again and they're sending someone out here in the morning. Someone from the fire service too. They want to find out exactly what caused the fire. They say it might not have been arson. It could have been an accident. The

dry weather we've been having was probably a contribu-
tory factor, they said. That's ironic, isn't it? We welcomed the sun to ripen the apples, and now they're trying
to say it destroyed everything. Where's the justice in
that?' She began to laugh hysterically until Bruce shook
her, then tears fell and he had to almost carry her
upstairs.

She did not sleep; she had known she wouldn't.
Coburn was lying. He had been out there, she had seen
him. So what sort of tale was he spinning the police?
He had the wealth and the power to get away with
anything.

At six she got washed and dressed and went downstairs. Bruce found her sitting in the kitchen staring out
at the blackened mass that had once been their pressing-
room.

'I'm going to sell up and move back to London,' she
said.

Bruce looked at her but said nothing, feeling the teapot
and then filling the kettle to make a fresh brew. He
popped bread into the toaster, and when it was ready he
sat down at the table beside her. 'I think that's a hasty
decision.'

'Can you think of a better one?' she snapped. 'I don't
see any point in living here without the cider farm. And
I'm unlikely to find a job that would suit me.'

'It can be rebuilt.'

'What with? The insurance money won't be enough.
The shed was so old it was worthless—and the press—
well, it will cost thousands for a new hydraulic one. No,
I might as well get rid of everything.'

'You're letting Coburn win?'

'I don't seem to have much choice,' she said. A
burning hatred raged inside her. 'But I shan't sell to him.

I'll put it on the market and find another buyer. If Coburn wants to negotiate with them afterwards, then that's his prerogative. At least I won't know anything about it.'

Bruce's eyes were solemn behind his tortoiseshell glasses. 'Don't do anything you might regret.'

She picked up a piece of toast and nibbled along one edge. 'I've had all night to think about it.'

'Yes, but you're angry. Give yourself a cooling-off period.'

Blythe tossed her head and pushed herself to her feet, walking over to the window and staring at the charred timbers. Her livelihood reduced to a pile of ashes! There were tears in her eyes when she turned. 'How could he do this to me?'

'Blythe, Coburn isn't the sort of character who'd do something like this out of spite.'

'Isn't he?' she demanded. 'We'd had one hell of a row only an hour earlier.'

Bruce's expression showed his surprise. 'I thought you were getting on well? What did you find to argue about?'

Blythe grimaced. 'You're never going to believe this. He's jealous of you.'

'*Me?* On what grounds?' he asked incredulously.

'The fact that we live together. His perverted little mind has us both in the same bed. According to Coburn, you're the reason I've not wanted to see him lately.'

'But that's nonsense. I hope you told him so?'

'Repeatedly, but he wouldn't believe me.'

Bruce shook his head and they finished their breakfast in silence. Afterwards they wandered outside to survey the damage. There was nothing left. Not one wall of the press-room left standing. Their apples were there, yes, because they had been housed in a separate brick building, unscathed by the fire, but of what use were they now?

The police inspector arrived, and a few minutes later the fire investigation officer. The ashes were carefully examined and some of them put into plastic bags to be taken away for further testing. Blythe invited the two men into the house for a cup of tea.

'Do you still believe it wasn't Coburn Daggart?' she asked the inspector.

'Obviously we can't be sure, not at this stage,' he said politely. 'But it would be totally out of character.'

'Did he deny he was here?'

'No. He admitted that, but——'

'There you are, then,' pounced Blythe. 'Of course it was him. I hope he gets all he deserves.'

Her blue eyes flashed her rage and Bruce touched her arm. 'Please, Blythe.'

She glared at him. 'Don't you see it has to be him? What was he doing out there? Why was he prowling around the yard? I hate that man!'

'Miss Berensen,' said the inspector, 'if it was Mr Daggart, then justice will be done, you can rest assured about that.'

'*If?*' she screamed. 'Of course it was him. If he's admitted he was here, then he's as good as said he did it. I want him arrested.'

The inspector looked at her sadly. 'The law doesn't work like that. We need proof. If you'd actually seen him drop a match or——'

'Well, I didn't. He was just walking around. Did he tell you why?'

'He said he was checking on your property because he feared the mysterious arsonist might be paying you a visit.'

'Mysterious arsonist, my foot,' she cried. 'That's a cover-up. If that was his reason he'd have knocked on my door and told me what he was doing. The fact that my house was in darkness probably told him I was in bed. And as Bruce's car wasn't here, he'd guess he was out. He picked his time perfectly.'

The inspector heaved a sigh and stood up. 'Don't worry, Miss Berensen, we'll examine all the facts. Whatever the truth is, we'll get to the bottom of it.'

When they had gone, Bruce said, 'Don't you think you're over-reacting?'

'No, I don't,' she snapped, 'and if you're on Coburn's side, then keep away from me.'

'I'm not on anybody's side,' he said, 'but without proof you haven't a leg to stand on.'

'I'll find it,' she cried, and she stormed out of the house. She went for a long walk, going over and over the facts in her mind, always coming up with the same answer, and she suddenly knew that she must see Coburn. Let him deny it to her face and she would—— Her thoughts faded. She would what? What could she do? She was nothing, a nobody compared to him. Who would believe her word against his? But she was still going to have it out with him.

She arrived at Druid's Cottage a few minutes before he got home from work. Smitty's face was harsh and unwelcoming when she saw Blythe, but she stood back and allowed the girl to enter. She knew, thought Blythe. Smitty knew she had accused Coburn of arson. Blythe was shown into his sitting-room and then left completely alone.

The Ferrari announced Coburn's arrival, and Blythe rose to face him. After a few minutes the door was pushed open and he stood there, his face granite-hard, his eyes fixed unnervingly on her.

But Blythe stood her ground. He was the one in the wrong. 'I think you know why I'm here?'

His jaw was tense and a muscle jerked in his cheek as he closed the door and leaned back against it. Blythe felt trapped. 'I imagine,' he said slowly, 'it's to make your accusation in person?'

'That's exactly right. You can't possibly get away with it. You do know that, don't you?'

'I think it's for the police to decide.'

Blythe wished he would stop looking at her. It was almost as though she was the one under suspicion.

'I don't think they've been able to find any proof.'

'Not yet,' she rasped. 'But since you didn't deny that you were there, it won't be long before they do.'

'I also told them the reason I was there.' He moved across the room and poured himself a Scotch, downing it in one swallow. The picture of a guilty man, thought Blythe.

'You'd check my property only minutes after arguing with me?' she sneered. 'If I believe that, I'll believe anything. You're so very sure of yourself. You think you're so very, very clever. But you won't get away with it, I'll make sure of that.'

'Really?' His brows rose. 'How?'

'I don't know yet, but I'll think of something,' she crisped. 'What are you hoping to gain out of it, that's what I'd like to know? You think I'll sell now? Was that the reason? Was that why you've been so nice to me lately? Do you know, you actually had me fooled. I was on the verge of saying I'd marry you. You did me a favour by showing your jealousy of Bruce. It's made me see what you're really like.'

He let her go on and on, no emotion at all on his chiselled face, and when she finally ran out of steam he said, 'If you've finished, I suggest you leave.'

'Yes, I have finished,' she said coldly. 'I just wanted you to know what I was feeling. But I doubt if the police have finished with you. I imagine you'll be hearing from them again—soon.'

When Blythe got back into her car she burst into tears, and it was several minutes before she composed herself sufficiently to drive home. And singing over and over in her mind were the words, I love him. I love him. Damn him, but I love him.

In bed that night she told herself it was impossible. How could she love a man who had such a rotten core? She was glad he had done what he did, because now she had proof that he was a typical Foxley-Daggart. And he deserved whatever it was he had coming to him.

CHAPTER TEN

BLYTHE could not believe it when Coburn sent word that
he was prepared to press her apples and pump the juice
into her own fermentation barrels. This did not sound
like the act of a man who had tried to destroy her.

She dismissed the messenger. 'Please tell Mr Daggart
I'll be in touch.' Then she went up to Bruce in his office
and told him what had happened.

'I'm not surprised,' he said. 'He's that type of man.
You're in trouble so he wants to help. The same as he's
helping me get off the ground. It proves you were wrong
to suspect him.'

Several days had gone by since the fire, and Blythe
had heard nothing more from the police. And deep down
in her heart of hearts, even though she did not want to
admit it, she knew Coburn was not responsible. He
would never seek revenge in such a manner simply because he thought she was two-timing him with Bruce.
Nor would he resort to such underhand methods to get
his hands on her land.

In the heat of the moment she had blamed him, but
he was a man of integrity, of honesty, of brutal truth if
necessary. He would never have done it. His explanation
as to why he had been on her property was probably a
true one. Such was his nature; he would still want to
protect her even though they had parted on such bad
terms.

'You're going to accept, of course?' Bruce's eyes were
upon her.

Her mouth twisted and she did not answer.

'You'd be a fool not to. He's casting you a lifeline. With the money you make out of this year's cider you'll be able to buy a new press.'

'I have my pride,' she said. 'I'm going to look a fool if I accept his help after I've accused him.'

'And how about Coburn's pride?' asked Bruce. 'How do you think he felt after you'd labelled him a criminal? I think the man must have a big heart.'

Blythe swallowed hard. 'I don't know what to do, Bruce.' She sat down on one of his chairs and looked soulfully into space. 'It would be a shame to let the apples rot, but accepting his help is tantamount to admitting that I don't believe he started the fire.'

He looked at her for a few long seconds. 'And do you, Blythe? Do you still believe it?'

She shrugged. 'I'm still waiting to hear what the police say.'

He shook his head, despairing of her. 'You'll destroy yourself, Blythe, if you go on like this. You're forgetting how well I know you. In fact, I think we ought to go out tonight. You need something to take your mind off your problems. We'll go to a movie in Taunton.'

Blythe did not really want to go, but she enjoyed the film and the drink afterwards, and when they got home she felt ten times better than she had in days.

'You were right, Bruce,' she said. 'I did need to get out. Thank you.' She kissed his cheek and he hugged her, and then suggested a hot chocolate before they went to bed.

A couple more days went by, and she was still unable to make up her mind whether to accept Coburn's offer, when he turned up in person. His red car screamed on to the drive and she was reminded of the day they had collided. It had been a volatile meeting and nothing seemed to have changed. Whenever they met, sparks flew. There had been a few idyllic weeks, but they had been short-lived, and she guessed they would never be able to recapture them.

She opened the door and stood back for him to enter. Bruce was in his office and she took Coburn through to her study. She knew why he was here. 'Tea? Coffee?'

'No, thanks,' he said.

'Please sit down.'

He obeyed, stretching his long legs out in front of him. 'Why aren't you taking up my offer? Can you afford to let your apples go to waste?'

'I'm surprised you asked me,' she said, frissons of awareness running through her. Would she ever be able to meet this man and not feel his power?

'I don't like to see anyone in trouble.'

Even a person who tried to blacken his name! Blythe knew she did not deserve any help. 'I really thought you were responsible——' ,

'Let's not discuss that,' he cut in peremptorily. 'I'm here purely in a business capacity. Do you want my help or not?'

'I'm not sure that I intend carrying on making cider,' she said. 'The insurance won't be enough to cover the cost of a new building, even supposing I could afford to buy a press.'

'You could have a loan. On the strength of what you told me about your order books, I'm sure no bank would refuse.'

Blythe frowned. Why was he being so helpful, so insistent that she carry on the business? 'I don't want to get into debt. I'm feeling my way. I could get into even more trouble than I am now.'

'You could accept a loan from me. Pay me back what you can, when you can. I'll even send round one of my accountants to advise you on how to look after your books.'

'Why?'

He let out an angry sigh. 'There's no ulterior motive, if that's what you're thinking. Good heavens, Blythe, won't you ever give me credit for doing something decent?'

'I'm sorry,' she said, avoiding his eyes and fiddling with a pencil on her desk. 'I just find it difficult to accept that you'll help me after the way I behaved.'

'I said I didn't want to talk about that. Do you want help, Blythe, or don't you?' He stood up and looked down at her. 'I'm a very busy man. If I'm wasting my time, just say so.'

Blythe rose too and made up her mind. 'Thank you, Coburn, I will accept your offer. Not money. But help with the apples. After the splash we made with the advertising campaign, it would be wrong not to honour the orders. They're still coming in, would you believe? I'll have to think about what I'm going to do next year.'

He nodded curtly and was gone, and the next thing Blythe knew a fleet of trucks came and collected both her store of apples and the barrels, which were also kept in another building and had miraculously escaped the fire.

Three days later the barrels came back filled with apple juice which would be left to ferment naturally before being racked for storage. The whole process would take about three months, and it would be Ben's job to keep a careful eye on the barrels.

She telephoned Coburn and thanked him for the trouble he had taken.

'Think nothing of it,' he said shortly, and put down the phone.

Bruce actually saw more of Coburn. He was nearing the end of his project now, and there was going to be television advertising as well as magazine and newspaper coverage. Druid's were introducing a completely new brand of cider, very light, and very much in tune with today's tastes. It could knock her sales for six. On the other hand, as their products were so completely different, it might have no effect. Whatever, Bruce had put equal amounts of time and effort into both advertising campaigns, and if they were both a success it would be to his credit.

She wanted to ask Bruce how Coburn was, but she was reluctant to show too much interest, and so she heard very little about him, except in a business sense. She wondered whether Coburn ever asked Bruce about her. He never said.

Autumn mists thickened the evening and morning air, dew glistened in woodland hollows, rosehips swelled and chestnuts grew in spiky green cases. Blythe watched a squirrel scampering up and down the branches of the horse-chestnut tree, chiselling at the shells until he broke them in half, carrying the nuts away to a private store.

The advertising campaign was a roaring success and Bruce's reputation began to grow. He talked about taking someone on to help him.

'How about me?' asked Blythe. 'I am an artist, in case you'd forgotten. Surely there's something I can do?' And it would take her mind off Coburn. She had more and more time on her hands, and often she did not know what to do with herself.

'Why didn't I think of that?' he asked. 'It really would be a big help.'

And so she spent her days drawing and conjuring up images to be discussed and thrown out by Bruce. He was a different man altogether when he was working. He knew what he wanted and would settle for nothing less. He was the same as Coburn in that respect.

It was eventually discovered that the arsonist who had started the other fires was to blame for hers. He had been caught at another farm in the area and confessed.

Blythe's overdue apology to Coburn could be put off no longer, and it came as a surprise and a disappointment when Bruce told her that he had gone to America for a month.

It was a reprieve, because, even though he had been big enough to offer help in her cidermaking, Blythe was not sure whether she was big enough to admit her mistake and ask his forgiveness.

He was the finest man she had ever met, she realised that now. He was nothing like his father or his grandfather or any of his other infamous antecedents. He was a caring man, and it was only because he loved her that he was jealous of Bruce. She should have seen that and made more effort to convince him he was mistaken.

If Coburn was away for a month, it meant he would be away for Christmas! Blythe suddenly realised that she had counted on seeing him then, if at no other time, it being a season of goodwill and all the rest of it. A perfect excuse for going to see him, or him coming to see her. Bruce was going home to his parents and she would be here alone.

Time had never dragged so slowly in her life. The weather grew cold and frosty, and when she went on her daily walks Blythe muffled herself up with plenty of thick sweaters and gloves and a scarf and boots. The countryside looked bleak. The trees were nothing more than skeletons. Autumn had gone out in a blaze of glory, and now there was nothing to look forward to except long, cold winter days.

Bruce went home on Christmas Eve. Blythe sat and watched television until late. Betty had invited her to Christmas dinner and she had accepted, unable to imagine anything worse than spending Christmas Day by herself.

At midnight the phone rang. She knew it would be Bruce. He had tried to persuade her to join him but she had refused. She picked up the receiver and a deep, familiar voice, which sent a thousand shivers down her spine, said, 'Merry Christmas, Blythe.'

For an instant she was too shocked to answer, then her whole being sprang into life. 'Merry Christmas, Coburn.' How thoughtful of him to ring all the way from America.

'I wasn't sure I'd find you in. I believe Bruce has gone to spend Christmas with his parents. I thought you might have gone with him?'

'No.'

'Because he didn't ask, or because you didn't want to?'

'I didn't want to.' Just the sound of his voice was tearing her apart.

'You're there alone?'

'Yes,' she whispered.

'And I'm here alone.'

Oh, this was awful. What was he trying to say? 'Have you no friends over there?'

'I'm home, Blythe.' He spoke softly. 'I couldn't bear the thought of Christmas in another country.'

Her heart leapt. 'How about Smitty?'

'Gone to her sister's.'

'Who's cooking your dinner?'

'Myself. Smitty's left me a list of unnecessary instructions. She seems to think I'm incapable.' He laughed shortly. 'I think I'd better let you get to bed. Goodnight, Blythe. Have a happy Christmas.'

'You too,' she said faintly.

The phone clicked and went dead, and she stood there holding it, feeling suddenly bereft. She wondered why he had phoned. It didn't make sense that he had just wanted to wish her the compliments of the season.

It took a few minutes for the answer to come to her. He was giving her another chance. He was asking her to go to him and put matters right between them. But could she do it? Was she strong enough? She loved him enough, that was for sure, and she knew he was not the trickster she had first thought him. But could she swallow her pride sufficiently to apologise, to again declare her love—and perhaps even ask him to marry her? She knew that it had to come from her.

Blythe went to bed and spent the night wrestling with her problem. The next morning she had made up her mind. She rang Betty and said she wouldn't be coming to dinner after all. The woman was surprised, but then cautiously pleased when Blythe said she would be spending the day with Coburn instead. With a bit of luck.

She dressed carefully in a new red woollen dress, and when she arrived at Druid's Cottage her heart was pounding fit to burst.

Coburn opened the door and stood for a couple of seconds looking at her. He wore black close-fitting trousers and a thin black cashmere sweater. He was un- smiling and looked forbidding, and Blythe almost turned tail and ran. She had made a mistake, a big mistake. He did not want her here at all.

'May I come in?' she whispered. If he hesitated much longer she really would go.

'Of course. I was just surprised to see you.' He stood back for her to enter, and as she walked past him Blythe breathed in his heady masculine scent. It filled her head, her lungs, her heart. How she loved this man. And how close she had come to losing him. Please God, let everything go right this morning, she prayed.

He took her coat and hung it up, and in his sitting-room a bottle of champagne nestled in a bucket of crushed ice. It was already open and a half-empty glass stood on the table beside it. She wondered if he always drank champagne for breakfast.

'To what do I owe this honour?' he asked, and there was no encouragement in his tone. It was as if he had never phoned and given her this opportunity to make amends.

'You—I——' Blythe looked down at her nervously twisting fingers. 'I came to wish you a Merry Christmas—in person. It's silly, isn't it, the two of us sitting in our houses alone?'

'I've done it before,' he said.

'I haven't. I've never been by myself at Christmas.'

'Then why did you turn down Bruce's invitation?'

'Because I didn't want to go.'

'You can bear to be parted?'

'I don't love Bruce,' she said quietly. 'Whatever you might think, we really are just good friends.' And she silently implored him to believe her.

'Sit down.' He indicated a chair and she dropped into it gratefully. Coburn sat too, stretching out his long legs before him, eyeing her thoughtfully but not speaking.

He was certainly not making things easy. What was she going to say? How could she broach the subject? She could not simply say that she wanted to marry him. There was the matter of the fire to be cleared up first.

'Coburn, about the fire,' she began hesitantly. 'I'm sorry I blamed you.'

'So am I,' he said. 'The police didn't give me a pleasant time.'

'I should have known you wouldn't do a thing like that.'

'Yes, you should.' His eyes were intent upon her face, unnerving her, making her almost give up. 'But then again, you've never trusted me, have you?'

Blythe closed her eyes and clenched her fists, taking a deep, steadying breath. 'I thought I had good reason.'

'Family traits and all that,' he thrust crisply.

She nodded. 'It happened so soon after we'd argued that I didn't stop to think clearly. Having seen you out there, I simply assumed it was you.'

'Why didn't you come and speak to me?'

'You'd gone when I got downstairs.' And then, in a painful whisper, 'They've caught the arsonist.'

'So I've heard,' he said drily.

'But I knew even before then that you weren't to blame.'

His blond brows rose. 'Thank goodness for that. What made you decide? When you came to see me you'd practically got me hung, drawn and quartered.'

'I'm so sorry,' she said. 'It was very wrong of me. You're not at all a vindictive type of person.'

'I'm glad you appreciate that.'

'You didn't have to salvage my apples. You made me feel awful, do you know that? I almost refused.'

'No, I didn't have to, did I?' he said crisply. 'In fact, it would have served you right if I'd sued you for slander instead. Do you still think I'm a louse? Do you still think I'm after your land?'

'No.' She shook her head firmly.

'Then what do you think?'

That I love you! 'I think I don't deserve your generosity. I think you're the kindest, most fair-minded person I've ever met, and it would serve me right if you never spoke to me again.'

'Would that upset you?'

Blythe could not look at him. Her throat was thick as she spoke. 'Yes, it would.'

'Why?'

'Because—because—I care about you.'

'Care about me?' He looked surprised. 'In what way?'

'Oh, Coburn, you're not making this easy. I love you. You know that.'

'No, I don't,' he said firmly. 'If you loved me, if you truly loved me, as you once said you did, then you would never have thought me capable of arson. I don't know what it is you think you feel for me, but it certainly isn't love.'

Blythe almost got up then and walked out. She was wasting her time. He wouldn't listen and she couldn't blame him. But her whole future happiness hinged on the outcome of this morning, so she must not give up, no matter how hard it became.

'Coburn, I made a mistake. A grave mistake. I was hurt because we'd argued over Bruce. I'm sorry. I'm truly sorry. Will you please forgive me?'

He looked at her long and hard, and then the flicker of a smile curved his lips. He pressed a fist to his chest. 'Something in here tells me I should. But my mind tells me to be wary. How about all the other things you've accused me of?'

Blythe went to him and knelt down. 'Please, Coburn.' Her heartbeats were erratic. This was her life she was pleading for. 'I promise I'll never suspect anything bad of you again.'

His narrowed eyes gave nothing away. 'You make it sound as though my forgiveness is important?'

'It is.' She went to clutch his hand, then backed away. 'Coburn, I really do love you and I—I want to marry you.'

These last words were said quickly, and she heard his swift intake of breath. 'Is that a proposal, Blythe?'

She swallowed her last remnants of pride and looked him squarely in the eyes. 'Yes, it is. I've wronged you, and in so doing I've hurt both you and myself. I can't go on like that any longer.'

'You know I would never have asked you again?'

She nodded.

'What if your attitude has killed my love for you?'

Blythe felt tears sting the backs of her eyes. It was no less than she deserved. 'I'd feel like half a person. I wouldn't want to live.'

'You're very much a whole person, Blythe,' he said softly. 'And I love you very much, too. And it should be I begging your forgiveness for being such a bastard over Bruce.'

'You believe now that he's never meant anything to me?'

He nodded. 'Yes, I do.' And he took her face between his palms. Blythe leaned towards him and his kiss was the most wonderful experience of her life. It was a promise of things to come. It was an act of forgiveness. It was a profession of love. And much more.

'I shouldn't be doing this,' he muttered thickly against her throat. 'I ought to put you over my knee and spank you for all the unhappiness you've caused.'

'I'll spend the rest of my life making it up to you,' she promised.

'No, I don't want you to do that.' He looked into her eyes and his smile was infinitely tender. 'I just want you to have faith in me, as I now have faith in you. I want you to be your own sweet self. To forget the past and live only for the future.'

He pulled her on to his lap and kissed her again, and Blythe wondered how she could ever have mistrusted this marvellously sensitive man.

'There is one thing that I think we should sort out before we get married,' he said at length.

'My cider farm?' she asked quietly.

He nodded, his face serious now. 'If you want to carry on making cider in your quaint, traditional way, then that's all right by me. I'll even get you a new press made.'

Blythe wondered whether it would ever really be a viable proposition. It would be a lot of hard work for very little results. Coburn's methods were so much more realistic. Unless they could combine the two? There had certainly been a lot of interest shown. Why back out when she was on to a winner?

'I'll tell you what,' she said. 'My land and farm buildings will be a wedding present to you on condition that you carry on making Berry's traditional cider.'

'That's a deal,' he grinned. 'How about the house?'

'I think we ought to let Bruce have that, for a nominal rent. It will be nice to have our advertising man right on our doorstep, don't you think?'

'You don't think he'll want to go back to London now there's no hope where you're concerned?'

'He always knew there was none,' she protested. 'And no, I don't think he will go back. He likes it here, and he's met a girl who he seems to think a lot of, so——'

'So I won't have to worry about him lusting after my wife?' he taunted, nibbling her ear.

Delicious shivers ran down Blythe's spine. 'There's only one man I want to lust after me, and he's right here.'

'And have I lot of lusting to catch up on,' he threatened.

She touched his mouth with the tip of her tongue, and he groaned and crushed her against him. 'Why did you come back from America so soon?' she asked. 'I understood you were to be away for a month.'

'And do you know why I went?'

Blythe shook her head.

'So that I couldn't possibly bump into you. I was afraid I would weaken. I wanted to hate you. Blythe, have you any idea of the agony I've gone through?'

'A little,' she whispered. If it was anywhere near hers.

'I came back because I couldn't stand it any longer. And Christmas gave me the excuse to phone you.'

'It was a last attempt for us to get back together?'

'Yes,' he said.

'I'm glad,' she whispered.

'Not half as glad as me. If you hadn't taken the bait, this would have been my worst Christmas ever.'

She smiled. 'Don't you think we ought to think about cooking dinner?'

His eyes lazily moved over her face. They were blue eyes at this moment, verging on grey, almost hidden by lowered lids. She thought they were the most beautiful eyes she had ever seen, and they did things to her that ought never to be allowed.

'If you really think that Christmas turkey is more important than me, then go ahead,' he said. 'I'm actually quite happy as I am.'

And, in all truthfulness, so was she. She snuggled closer to him, and that was how they sat for the next hour. Or maybe it was two. Neither of them knew. Time had lost all meaning.

HARLEQUIN
Romance

Coming Next Month

#3031 THE ASKING PRICE Amanda Browning
Sian wants to leave the past behind, but Blair Desmond. her attractive new boss, blames her for the death of his friend. He is wrong, of course, but even if he'd listen to her explanations, would he believe her?

#3032 RED HOT PEPPER Roz Denny
Take a stubborn redhead named Pepper Rivera and a rakish but charming major named Dev Wade. Add two matchmaking fathers, five overprotective brothers, one flashy sports car and an overgrown sheepdog. Then wait for the sparks—and the fur—to fly.

#3033 WHEN WE'RE ALONE Jane Donnelly
Corbin is a persistent investigative reporter, and Livvy finds it hard not to fall under his spell. The more involved they become, the harder it is to keep any secrets from him. And there's one secret he simply must never discover....

#3034 ISLAND DECEPTION Elizabeth Duke
Gemma's relaxing holiday on the Great Barrier Reef while getting over her broken engagement is spoiled by her clashes with resident doctor Chad Rivers—who thinks Gemma is an empty-headed model. And Gemma isn't about to tell him that she is a doctor, too.

#3035 QUEEN OF HEARTS Melissa Forsythe
On her way to Nice to play in an international bridge tournament Nikki Damon learns that you can't bring a fantasy to life—in her case, by kissing a handsome stranger in Paris—and expect to walk away, as if it never happened.

#3036 NO NEED TO SAY GOODBYE Betty Neels
If Louise ever thinks about Dr. Aldo van der Linden, it is as a professional colleague, not as a man. Until the day he involves himself in the affairs of her family, particularly her sister Zoe. Somehow, Louise finds it difficult to be pleased.

Available in February wherever paperback books are sold, or through Harlequin Reader Service:

In the U.S.
901 Fuhrmann Blvd.
P.O. Box 1397
Buffalo, N.Y. 14240-1397

In Canada
P.O. Box 603
Fort Erie, Ontario
L2A 5X3

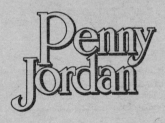

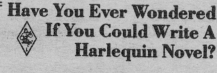

Have You Ever Wondered If You Could Write A Harlequin Novel?

Here's great news—Harlequin is offering a series of cassette tapes to help you do just that. Written by Harlequin editors, these tapes give practical advice on how to make your characters—and your story—come alive. There's a tape for each contemporary romance series Harlequin publishes.

Mail order only

All sales final

TO: **Harlequin Reader Service**
Audiocassette Tape Offer
P.O. Box 1396
Buffalo, NY 14269-1396

I enclose a check/money order payable to HARLEQUIN READER SERVICE® for $9.70 ($8.95 plus 75¢ postage and handling) for EACH tape ordered for the total sum of $_____.*
Please send:

☐ Romance and Presents   ☐ Intrigue
☐ American Romance   ☐ Temptation
☐ Superromance   ☐ All five tapes ($38.80 total)

Signature_____

Name:_____ (please print clearly)

Address:_____

State:_____ Zip:_____

*Iowa and New York residents add appropriate sales tax.

AUDIO-H

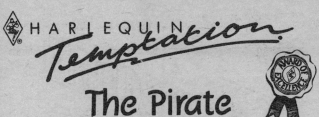

HARLEQUIN Temptation

The Pirate
JAYNE ANN KRENTZ

At the heart of every powerful romance story lies a legend. There are many romantic legends and countless modern variations on them, but they all have one thing in common: They are tales of brave, resourceful women who must gentle and tame the powerful, passionate men who are their true mates.

The enormous appeal of Jayne Ann Krentz lies in her ability to create modern-day versions of these classic romantic myths, and her LADIES AND LEGENDS trilogy showcases this talent. Believing that a storyteller who can bring legends to life deserves special attention, Harlequin has chosen the first book of the trilogy—THE PIRATE—to receive our Award of Excellence. Look for it in February.

AE-PIR-1

Harlequin Historicals®

Step into a world of pulsing adventure, gripping emotion and lush sensuality with these evocative love stories penned by today's bestselling authors in the highest romantic tradition. Pursuing their passionate dreams against a backdrop of the past's most colorful and dramatic moments, our vibrant heroines and dashing heroes will make history come alive for you.

Watch for new Harlequin Historicals each month, available wherever Harlequin Books are sold.

History has never been so romantic!

GHIST-1R